HOT TEA AND A COLD CASE

TEA TIME COZY MYSTERIES, BOOK 2

SUMMER PRESCOTT

SUMMER PRESCOTT BOOKS PUBLISHING

Copyright 2021 Summer Prescott Books

All Rights Reserved. No part of this publication nor any of the information herein may be quoted from, nor reproduced, in any form, including but not limited to: printing, scanning, photocopying, or any other printed, digital, or audio formats, without prior express written consent of the copyright holder.

**This book is a work of fiction. Any similarities to persons, living or dead, places of business, or situations past or present, is completely unintentional.

CHAPTER ONE

Laney dunked the last piece of her French toast in the rich maple syrup that had pooled on her plate, savoring the last delightful tidbit of the homemade breakfast that had been offered that day at The Evergreen Bed and Breakfast. Wiping her mouth with the white cloth napkin, she looked up as a man entered the room, his familiar smile making butterflies flutter madly in her midsection.

"Raymond? What are you doing here?" she asked, chasing her last bite of breakfast with a swig of coffee.

"I could ask you the same thing," Raymond chuckled. "The hiking is great up here, so when I have a little bit of time after a rough week, every so often, I come up to recharge. Are you staying here?"

"Yep, got in last night. Those feather beds are amazing. I felt like I was sleeping on a cloud." Laney smiled dreamily. "I was just about to hit one of the hiking trails, now that I'm done with breakfast. Maybe you could show me around," she suggested, hoping that she wasn't giving him the wrong idea.

While Laney found Raymond, the Mayor of Iberden, to be attractive, she was nowhere near ready to be in a relationship and wasn't even considering dating yet. The breakup that had driven her to leave New York behind and move to a small town in Vermont was still too fresh in her mind.

"I'd be happy to," Ray agreed immediately. "I need to gather up a few things before I hit the trail, but maybe I could meet you back down here in say..." He looked at his phone to check the time. "Fifteen minutes?"

"Perfect. I'll go grab my gear and see you in a few." Laney nodded.

It would actually be nice, and a ton safer, having someone to hike with. Anything could happen on the trail and having someone there to help deal with any emergency that might arise would be smart.

Laney hurried back to her delightfully cozy guest room, tossed her hair into a quick messy bun, donned her new hiking boots, grabbed her backpack, and headed for the foyer just outside the B&B's breakfast room. She hadn't been there for more than a couple of minutes, when she saw Ray trotting down the stairs, his hand on the ornate antique rail.

"All set?" he asked, his backpack slung over one shoulder.

"I think so." Laney nodded. "It's been quite a while since I've been hiking, but I figured it would be tragic for me to live this close to such beauty and not go out and take a look at it."

"I totally agree. Iberden has its drawbacks – the tough winters, everyone knowing everyone's business, the lack of a decent bookstore – but when you get to the waterfalls on the Centennial Trail, you'll see that it's totally worth putting up with all of that." Ray smiled.

Laney's mouth fell open. "There's a waterfall?" she whispered.

Ray laughed at her reaction. "One of the most beautiful waterfalls in the state," he promised. "There's a trail that I like to use, just outside of the Centennial Woods, which is only a 20 minute drive from here. It'll take us right to it. We'll be heading up to the waterfall by 10 am at the latest."

"I'll definitely want to hang out there for a while to get some pictures," Laney mused, filled with anticipation. "I need to make sure I get some material for my next project while we're there."

"Absolutely. The views up there are spectacular," Raymond assured her. "You'll get some great shots, I have no doubt. I have all day and you can spend as much time as you want on your photography gig."

Laney laughed. "You're going to regret saying that. You should definitely impose a time limit, or we might end up camping out in the woods tonight by the time I'm satisfied with the pictures."

"Have a nice trip back," Raymond teased. "Because after all of that exercise and fresh air, I'm going to be heading back here for a nice steak dinner and maybe a soak in the hot tub."

Laney chuckled, then turned towards the front door of the B&B. "Yeah, I think a steak dinner sounds better than camping in the woods and subsisting on Pop Tarts, so lead the way."

There was one other family staying at The Evergreen this weekend, and they weren't up for breakfast yet, so Laney and Raymond passed the deserted small dining room, which reminded Laney an awful lot of her own place, Marcy's Tea Room, back in Iberden. Small tables, painted in different colors, dotted a room filled with bright rugs, and there were eclectic paintings on the walls, creating a warm coziness that Laney loved.

She had inherited her late grandmother's Tea Room and revived it – freshening up the interior with new paint, sumptuous rugs, and her personal paintings. Now, it was more lively than it had been in years. There were the Iberden regulars, who came in around the same time every day and ordered nearly the same thing every time, and then there were the tourists. Iberden was a picturesque small town that had something to offer out of town guests year-round, so business stayed brisk.

Laney had even been able to hire a part-time server, Carly, who also worked at the thrift store in town where Laney had found many of her sets of silver and random teacups. Carly was such a dear that she'd practically shoved Laney out the door on Friday, with strict orders not to come back until she'd had some fun. Laney felt a little bit guilty about leaving the young lady in charge, but knew that she was capable, so she tried to not worry...too much.

Raymond held the passenger door of his car open and closed it after Laney was seated. She was beyond glad that he was doing the driving, so that she was free to gaze dreamily out of the window, taking in the stunning vistas around her. Raymond drove in silence, allowing her to focus on the experience, until he pulled into the parking lot of what appeared to be an old-fashioned general store.

"Oh, wow - this is so cute!" Laney exclaimed, loving the rustic wooden exterior that had a wagon wheel fence on either side of the double doors that led inside. "What are we doing here?"

"Last stop before the trail – this is where we stock up on snacks and water," Raymond replied. "They have trail mix, granola bars, and the best beef jerky you'll ever taste." He turned the car off and Laney followed him inside, breathing in deeply the fragrant mountain air. There were a few other people in the quaint little shop, walking around browsing the camping gear, but Raymond and Laney made a beeline for the snacks and the coolers where the water bottles were kept.

"'Morning, folks," a chipper older man greeted them when they reached the front counter with their bounty. "Can I help you with anything?"

"Nope, I think we found everything we need," Raymond replied, setting down his items and making room for Laney's.

"Well, it sure does look like you guys found everything alright." He chuckled, scanning the items. "I'm Ed, by the way, the owner - my store has been the main stop before and after hitting the trails, for ages." Raymond handed him a credit card before Laney could protest and paid for all the items. Ed ran it and handed it back to him. "Going to Centennial Woods, I suppose?"

"Actually," Raymond replied, "I found another trail that I wanted to hit today. It's a little less touristy and it runs alongside a couple of the Centennial Woods trails."

"Ah, yes, I think you're referring to Baker's Point," Ed interrupted. "Definitely a hidden gem, but make sure you follow the trail markers - unfortunately that trail hasn't been managed for a while since it's so quiet."

"Thanks for the tip," Raymond grinned and headed back to the car.

Once they were back on the road, Laney loaded her snacks and water into her pack and was just zipping it up when they pulled into the little three-car parking lot with the wooden sign out front alerting them they had arrived at Baker's Point Preserve.

"You didn't need to buy my snacks you know." She raised an eyebrow at Raymond.

"Of course, I didn't have to, I wanted to." He grinned impishly. "Maybe if you're really nice, I'll let you buy me dinner as a thank you."

"Oh, I see how it is. You buy granola bars and I buy a steak dinner? Somehow I'm thinking that's not going to work." Laney laughed.

"Well, they are very good granola bars." Raymond pretended to pout and when Laney burst into laughter, he couldn't help himself and joined in. "Seriously though, don't worry about it. I'm just glad for company on the trail, it was my pleasure to buy snacks for a hiking companion."

"Well then, thank you. I'll have you know, I'm pretty fast, so if we encounter a bear..." Laney warned.

"I'll be the snack and not you?" Raymond laughed.

"I'm just saying..."

They got out of the car and Ray quickly tossed his share of the snacks into his backpack. While he was putting on his pack, Laney wandered over to do a quick check of the map over by the trail head.

"I'm sorry," she shook her head, perplexed. "I can't make heads nor tails of this thing."

"Yeah, it's a little confusing with the cross-country skiing maps superimposed, but don't worry, I've been here before. We're just going to follow the trees that have blue dots on them."

He traced the line of the blue trail with his finger. "Up to the falls and back down," Ray finished, tracing the path back to where they were starting. He glanced at his watch and seemed to be calculating something.

"We're probably looking at a good two hours each way. It's just about ten o'clock now, so plan on taking your photos around noon as long as we don't dilly dally."

Laney nodded, tucked a loose strand of hair behind her ear, and bounded excitedly toward the trail, Raymond following close behind. She was pleasantly surprised to find that she wasn't as completely out of shape as she thought she might have been, and she was able to keep up the pace for the first hour and a half with no problems at all. Yes, they stopped briefly for water and a snack, but Laney felt energized with each step she took, particularly when she started hearing running water up ahead. After a sharp turn to the right, Laney's jaw dropped, and she froze in place as the breathtakingly gorgeous waterfall came into view. She had no idea that Raymond was standing beside her until he spoke. "Beautiful isn't it?" he asked, gazing at the falls.

"Beautiful doesn't even begin to describe it," Laney breathed.

She set her backpack on the ground and rummaged through it to find her camera. Fiddling with a selection of lenses, she finally found just the right one and scurried away to start taking pictures, leaving Raymond standing alone by the edge of the path. Laney wandered further behind the waterfall, hoping to get a good shot from a different angle. She was standing in the alcove of stone behind the falls, watching Raymond's blurry profile on the other side of the water when she decided to try to climb just a little way up the rocky wall to get a better shot. She was almost up to the right vantage point when a few of the rocks gave way beneath her feet, sending her tumbling to the ground.

"Laney!" Raymond sprinted toward her.

Relieved that nothing but her pride had been hurt, Laney stood up, brushed off her backside, and turned to Raymond to tell him she was OK, but found him squinting into the pile of rubble that had come down from the wall. Then he pointed and crouched down to get a better look.

"Are those…bones?" He frowned.

Laney squatted beside him and looked down at what she previously thought were loose rocks that had fallen. There were indeed pieces of bone scattered in the mixture. She shuddered. Getting involved in one murder investigation since she came to Iberden had been bad enough, but now it seemed like she might just be headed for a second one. With any luck, the bones were simply from animals, but something in her gut told her that wasn't the case.

CHAPTER TWO

"I can't be sure yet," Detective Worth said, "but I think this could be linked to that cold case back in the nineties."

"From Iberden?" an older man in a Park Service uniform asked. "I was the head ranger back then too. We worked with the police and sheriff and sent out search parties for a week looking for that poor girl and found nothing."

Detective Worth crossed her arms over her chest. "Yet somehow these two," she pointed to Laney and Raymond, "may have just uncovered the evidence by accident?" She looked skeptical. "Seems like the search wasn't up to par back then," she muttered to herself, shaking her head.

"I wouldn't say that's an accurate assessment, ma'am. We did the best we could with the resources that we had," Mr. Dale, the park ranger, insisted, looking a bit hot under the collar. "We were terribly under-staffed back then, and so was local law enforcement. We don't get those kinds of crimes out here, so we're not set up for them." His brow furrowed. "We had to cover all of Centennial Woods and the connecting trails with that bare-bones team."

Detective Worth arched an eyebrow at his litany of excuses. "I'm not blaming you or your team, Mr. Dale, I'm just stating the facts. This story is going to be all over the news if we confirm that the bones are linked to that case. You need to make sure that you're prepared for the scrutiny that you'll be under from the press, because acting defensively isn't going to get us anywhere."

With that, she turned to face Laney. "Ms. Powers." Detective Worth put her hands on her hips. "*How* on earth did you and Mr. Andrews get wrapped up in something like this again?"

Laney opened her mouth to reply, but Worth held up a finger to silence her. "Never mind," the detective said shaking her head. "Just go home and try to forget that you saw any of this. The last thing we need is the news leaking before we have a chance to confirm the evidence. Am I being fairly clear?" She gave them a meaningful look, brows raised.

Raymond, ever the politician, answered before Laney had a chance to speak. "Yes, Detective, we hear you loud and clear. Trust me, we don't want to be involved in this at all, so we'll just head back to Iberden and pretend it never happened, right Laney?"

"Oh! Uh...yeah, of course. I've had just about enough of bodies and bones and investigations since I came to town," she agreed, nodding vehemently. "We'll definitely stay out of your way, Detective."

Laney turned to Raymond. "Let's head back to The Evergreen," she suggested.

Raymond nodded and started down the trail, with Laney close behind.

"Hey, do you think that we could stop at The Country Store on the way back to The Evergreen? I'd like to at least get some sort of souvenir since my trip got cut short," Laney asked, after they were buckled in and pulling out of the parking lot, having hiked double-time to get back to the car.

"Um, I guess..." Raymond frowned. "But do you *really* want something to remember this trip? We didn't even really have a chance to hike Baker's Point."

Laney shrugged, though she knew Raymond didn't see her, since he was focused on driving. She figured that her lack of response would suffice and sure enough, Raymond slowed down when they reached the old wooden sign for The Country Store and turned into the parking lot. "Come on." He smiled. "Let's go get your souvenir."

As soon as they walked through the door and the bell jingled, Ed greeted them. "Ah, the cute couple who wanted to go on the less traveled path. How'd the hike go?"

Blushing to the roots of her hair at the older man's assumption, Laney didn't want to be rude, so she blurted out a reply. "We had fun!" She forced a smile. "Now we're back for a souvenir before we head home."

Ed looked from Laney to Raymond, as if he had detected that something was wrong, but couldn't figure out what. Laney hoped he wouldn't press the issue. She wanted to get in, get her souvenir and get out.

"What's your hurry? Did you even get to head over to Centennial Woods, by the real touristy spots? There's some fun stuff to see over there, that's why it's so popular."

Feeling trapped, Laney coughed out an awkward laugh and looked desperately at Raymond for help. He got the hint.

"Oh, no Ed, we didn't get a chance to head over there before we had to leave," Raymond replied smoothly. "I think they were actually closing off Centennial Woods and Baker's Point for the day right when we finished up our first hike. Didn't get to do the whole path, but we got some nice pictures all the same."

Ed raised his eyebrows. "Oh?" He crossed his arms over his chest and tilted his head. "They say what was going on? Some sort of event or a party or something?"

Laney remained silent, pretending to be suddenly fascinated by a display of chewing gum, but Raymond saved the day once again. "Not sure." He shrugged. "Something with the park ranger, Mr. Dale..."

Ed looked distracted, staring behind Raymond and Laney as Raymond replied. Curious, Laney turned to the door and noticed police cars driving by, away from Baker's Point, with the park patrol vehicle following.

"Oh my..." Ed frowned. "I hope no one got hurt."

Laney tried to feign surprise and match Ed's concern. "I guess it's a good thing we're going home now." She nudged Raymond, who was still looking out the door where Detective Worth's car had just passed by moments ago. Raymond startled at her touch but recovered quickly.

"You know Ed," he spoke up a bit to recapture the shopkeeper's attention. "We really should be going, but how about you recommend a nice souvenir for us to pick up on our way out?"

Ed was obviously concerned, but clearly tried his best to shake it off so that he could be of service to his customers. He snapped into sales mode and pulled a couple of mugs from under the counter. They had "Centennial Woods" printed across the front and each was a different color.

"Oh, they're great," Laney manufactured some enthusiasm, eager to be on her way. "I'll take the purple one."

She pulled out her wallet and placed her credit card in the machine after Ed rang it up. He wrapped it agonizingly carefully in tissue paper and gently placed it in a paper bag along with the receipt before finally handing it to Laney.

"Please, tell your friends about this place too. We always love visitors." He turned to Raymond and handed him a business card, which Ray tucked into his pocket.

"Will do." He nodded to the friendly shop owner.

Laney didn't relax until they were out of the store and back into the car.

"I don't like that we had to lie to him," she admitted with a sigh.

"It's better that he finds out with official news like everyone else. Worth warned us not to say anything about it," Raymond replied, starting the car, and heading for The Evergreen. "Are you planning to stay the night at the B&B again?" he asked, changing the subject.

"I had planned on it, but after all of the excitement, I think I'm just going to pack my things and head home." Laney leaned her head back against the seat.

"What about you?" she asked, glancing over at Raymond, who appeared to be lost in thought.

"Yeah, same here." He nodded. "This was supposed to be a restful weekend, but that's definitely not happening, so I might as well pack it up."

Laney made a commiserating sound, then leaned forward to turn up the radio and tried to relax for the rest of the ride back to the B&B.

CHAPTER THREE

Laney scanned the local newspaper the morning after she returned to Iberden, but when she saw that the front-page story was about the fall festival next weekend, she quickly scrolled through the news on her phone and surprisingly found absolutely nothing about the human bones that had been discovered near the waterfall. Though she felt like she should let out a sigh of relief, she just couldn't relax. The memory of the bones scattered about her feet haunted her and though she knew that she needed to just forget she'd ever seen them, she just... couldn't.

With a sigh, she finally admitted to herself that there was no way that she'd be able to let go of the memories until she at least did some investigating of her own. She'd have to dig into the cold case that Detective Worth had mentioned at least a bit. It felt irresponsible to just leave it alone. Those bones had belonged to someone, and as the person who discovered them, Laney felt strongly compelled to do something.

The morning rush hadn't started in Marcy's Tea Room yet. The regulars usually descended en masse beginning around nine o'clock. Carly was getting things ready in the back - Laney could hear trays being pulled from the holding racks, and the water running in the sink - but other than that, she was alone at her little table in the corner. Ever since she'd seated herself at that particular table, on the first day that she'd first arrived in Iberden, the corner table had been her go-to spot.

She took a good-sized bite of the lemon muffin that she'd filched from the kitchen and washed it down with a delicate orange pekoe tea, sitting for a moment and just taking in the cozy appeal of the shop. One of the perks of owning a tea shop was having a seemingly endless supply of teas from all over the world to sample and enjoy in an environment that instantly made her relax and feel good.

Just as her grandmother had, Laney served nothing but the finest teas, and all of the goodies that went along with them were homemade, using the highest quality ingredients.

So much had happened in that cozy room, over the first few months. Laney would never forget the rocky start to her new life in Iberden – after all, it's rather hard to dismiss the memory of having a dead mayor in one's parlor – but, aside from that, it hadn't taken long for her to settle into her new hometown and get the Tea Room up and running again, just like her beloved grandma would've wanted.

She was surrounded by new friends who felt like family, and fully realized that she was intentionally keeping dear Raymond at arm's length. The breakup that she'd had before moving to Vermont had affected her profoundly, and her bruised heart wasn't even close to ready to try again with someone new. Yet.

Everything in the quaint small town was so different from her formerly rushed and stressed out life in New York City, but the fact that she'd encountered evidence of yet another murder in the pastoral hamlet certainly seemed odd and gave her pause for thought. Laney jumped, suddenly jarred from her thoughts by the jingling of the bells over the front door.

She looked up and smiled when she saw Babby, the elderly owner of the best antique shop in town walking in, followed closely by Raymond. Babby's shop had played a huge role in Laney's plan to redecorate the Tea Room. Her grandmother had made the large Victorian home a grand place that felt very formal, but Laney wanted everyone to feel comfortable in the Tea Room, so she had added some whimsical touches – tables with mismatched chairs painted in soft colors, and curtains in fun, colorful fabrics. She'd bought mismatched tea sets and silver pieces from Babby, along with several sumptuous rugs.

Babby and Raymond took their seats at Laney's table, ready for what had become a fairly regular occurrence shortly after the Tea Room had opened its doors once again. The three of them would sit, chat, and try out the new teas and snacks, before the Tea Room opened for the day. Since Babby and Raymond were among the first people that Laney had met when she came to Iberden, they had taken her under their wings and had become very special to her. She also loved using them as guinea pigs to try out new recipes for the baked goods and special treats that she created for the Tea Room.

Owning and operating Marcy's Tea Room was by far the most fulfilling job that Laney had ever taken on. Yes, she loved her freelance art projects, but this path allowed her to explore her art in a new way. She showcased her pieces in the Tea Room, and had sold several, both to tourists and locals alike. When the locals discovered that Laney had created the paintings, photos, and sculptures, they lined up to commission new work.

She loved the fact that she could still be the free-spirited young woman whom her parents had shunned when she dropped out of college, while also managing to run her own successful business. She also couldn't help but wonder if her parents would think differently of her now that she'd chosen to follow a more traditional path. Laney shook off those questions - she didn't have the luxury of that type of thinking, thoughts like those would only rip open wounds that were barely covered with scars as it was.

"Ooh, new scones today?" Babby's eyes lit up when Carly brought out their sample platter for the morning.

"Yup." Laney smiled "Cranberry-orange, and cheddar-chive. I wanted to test out a new savory option along with a sweet one."

She picked up one of each from the serving plate and placed them on her dish, next to the pile of lemon crumbs that were all that remained of her muffin. Babby did the same, and Raymond took two of each, as usual. He always insisted that he needed to try them twice before he could make a fair decision, though Laney was pretty sure he always just showed up hungry.

"Laney." Babby swallowed a bite of scone and dabbed at her mouth with a napkin. "I want to hear all about your relaxing weekend, and I have to catch you up with what happened here while you were gone."

"I had a great time, Babby." Laney smiled, feeling a bit sick at having to carry out another deception. "The scenery was beautiful, the B&B was cozy and comfy, the food was great - there's just not that much else to tell, other than the fact that I ran into

Raymond up there. Turns out that he was staying at the exact same Bed and Breakfast. We went hiking together."

Laney focused on her scones like her life depended on it, to avoid making eye contact.

"Oh really?" Babby's eyebrows shot skyward. "Well, isn't that quite the coincidence?" she asked, glancing from Laney to Raymond and back again.

"Yes, and that's all it was…a coincidence." Laney gave the would-be-matchmaker a pointed look.

Babby tittered but didn't push the subject. "Well, I expect to see some pictures of the hike at least," she insisted, before starting on her own long-winded recap of every second that Laney missed at Marcy's Tea Room that weekend. Laney smiled and nodded at all the right times, but her mind wandered a bit until Babby mentioned Roger and Janet.

"They dropped by yesterday afternoon, just before you got back. I was finishing a lovely blend of orange and black pekoe, with just a touch of ginger, when they came in. I said hello and they stopped to chat for a bit. Turns out that they just had some time to visit this week and didn't know you were away. Roger has been staying with Janet to help her with some chores out at her place, but he said he'd be coming back to the Tea Room soon." Babby shrugged. "I figured they'd call your cell when I told them you weren't coming back until Sunday."

Laney was gripped by a sudden pang of guilt. Roger, her late grandmother's fiancé, had lived in the upstairs rooms of the Tea Room with Grandma Marcy, and he'd still been there when Laney arrived, after her grandmother's death. She'd told him that he'd always have a home in the Tea Room as long as she owned it. His granddaughter, Janet, who had been the attorney that handled Marcy's legal affairs, lived in a little house on the outskirts of town.

Roger and Janet had helped Laney get through the craziness that ensued after Mayor Andrews' murder, and since then, she had considered them family. Even though Grandma Marcy was no longer with her, having Roger and Janet, people who remembered her fondly, to talk to provided some measure of comfort.

"Not a problem, Babby." Laney gave her elderly friend a reassuring smile. "I'll give them a call later today. Maybe we can all get together this week for dinner," she suggested.

Babby nodded, took the last bite of her crumbly, savory scone, and wiped her mouth with a hand-embroidered lavender napkin.

"Delicious as always," she proclaimed, satisfied, smiling at Carly when she took away the plates. "I think I prefer the cheddar-chive, but the cranberry-orange is yummy too. I think you should serve both as the specials for today." Babby stood, taking the napkin from her lap, and placing it on the table. "I have a busy day today and about a thousand errands that I don't want to run, but I'll try to stop by later this afternoon for a cup of tea."

"Sounds like you'll need one," Laney teased, smiling fondly at her friend.

"You got that right," Babby muttered, sliding her chair back into place. She gave Laney and Raymond each a hug before shrugging back into her coat and strolling outside into the pale rays of the early winter sunshine, bells jingling as the door opened and shut.

Laney walked Raymond to the door and flipped the sign from Closed to Open, letting the town know that Marcy's Tea Room was officially open for the day. She greeted each customer with a wide smile and played the role of hostess, showing locals and tourists alike to their tables - her favorite task. The morning flew by and before Laney realized it, Babby was tapping her on the shoulder as she added up register receipts. Startled, Laney jumped.

"Sorry dear, didn't mean to scare you," Babby laughed, her eyes sparkling. "But since I'm the only one here, I'd be happy to watch over things while you take a little break if you'd like," she offered.

"Yep, Babby and I can take on the world," Carly piped up with a grin, taking a break from clearing tables and swinging her towel like a feather boa.

Laney laughed. "You two are the best – thank you. I believe I will take a break for a bit. I'll just be upstairs, so be sure to come and get me if you need an extra set of hands."

"Go on with you now," Babby shooed her away, giving Carly a conspiratorial grin. "We've got this."

"How can I argue with that?" Laney chuckled, untying her frilly apron, and heading for the stairs.

Once she was in her room and the door was closed, Laney went to her desk and opened her laptop. Finally. She clicked on the search engine tab and when it popped up on her screen, she began to type, *Iberden murder 1990s.* Laney was surprised when the search returned no results, but then she remembered that the cold case the detective mentioned had been about a missing girl. *Iberden missing girl 1990s,* she corrected. Now, there were twelve results and Laney knew from a look at the first page that she was on the right track. *Evelyn Mattis, 22, reported missing on June 13, 1992...*

CHAPTER FOUR

The rest of the day flew by. Carly closed the Tea Room by herself, though Laney had offered to help, so Laney had been able to read story after story, regarding the puzzling case of Evelyn Mattis, and before she knew it, the sun was already setting. When she heard a knock at the front door, Laney glanced at the corner of her laptop and noticed it was almost 8 pm. Her stomach growled, alerting her to the fact that, yet again, she'd skipped dinner. Ignoring her protesting stomach, she hurried down the stairs and opened the door. She was more than a bit taken aback and wondered if something had happened when she saw Raymond Andrews standing on her porch, holding a bright and cheerful bouquet of flowers.

"Ummm…what's going on?" she asked, with a frown, glancing from Raymond to the flowers and back again.

"A little birdie told me that it was your birthday tomorrow, so I'm taking you out to dinner," Raymond grinned, thrusting the flowers toward her.

"I told Babby not to tell anyone." Laney sighed, reluctantly taking the flowers. "I don't usually celebrate my birthday, and Ray, this is really sweet of you, but I've told you…I'm not looking for a relationship right now."

"I'm just taking you out to dinner, Laney. Think of me as a friend. I'd be a really bad friend if I didn't at least give you a good meal on your birthday eve," Raymond grinned, his adorable dimple making an appearance.

Laney was about to protest when her stomach growled audibly. She giggled at the betrayal, covering her midsection with her free hand.

"See, your stomach wants to go out to dinner," Raymond teased. "Come on now, I made reservations, so go put something pretty on and get ready for a lovely, no-romance, no-strings attached dinner. Deal?"

Laney looked down at her sweatpants, over-sized t-shirt, and mismatched socks, and laughed. "What, you don't think this is pretty enough?" she deadpanned.

"You look fabulous without even trying." Raymond grinned. "If you want to go to dinner just as you are, I'll happily take you."

Laney gave him a onceover. He looked amazing in freshly pressed trousers, a white button-down shirt, and a tweed blazer, under his full-length wool coat.

"I believe you would." Laney shook her head. "But even when I go out with friends, I make more of an effort than this, so you'll have to wait for a bit."

She let Raymond in and directed him to make himself at home, then trotted up the stairs and started sifting through her closet for an appropriate dress that wouldn't send the wrong message. Raymond was very sweet, but she'd meant what she said – now was not the time to even think about a relationship.

A simple, but elegant, black dress was shoved way in the back, as Laney rarely dressed up these days and it still had the tags on it. Thankfully it wasn't wrinkled. She pulled it on quickly, then bent down to check under the bed for her only pair of heels and slipped them on, feeling odd. She had dressed like this pretty regularly when she was a city girl in New York, but now she felt decidedly out of practice.

Her wardrobe since relocating to Vermont had mostly consisted of her paint-stained shirt and canvas shoes, with jeans, unless she was working in the Tea Room, and even then she wore tailored black trousers and a simple white blouse. She tossed her hair into a messy bun, dabbed on a bit of lip gloss, and didn't even take a final look in the full-length mirror before she grabbed her purse and trotted down the stairs to meet Raymond. The sooner she was ready, the sooner she'd be able to eat and then get home to do more research into the Evelyn Mattis case.

Raymond was waiting by the door and had just glanced at his watch as Laney made her entrance. When he looked up, for a moment he said nothing, seeming to tremendously enjoy watching her glide down the stairs. "Wow, you look amazing," he said softly, then seemed to deliberately shake off his reaction. "It only took you seven minutes, that's way better than I expected." He laughed.

"Sorry, got distracted." She grinned and grabbed her coat from the foyer closet, shrugging into it.

"I know the feeling," Raymond said so lightly that Laney wasn't sure that he'd said it at all. "Let's go enjoy a birthday dinner." He offered his arm, and, not wanting to trip since she was out of practice with high heels, Laney took it.

"Yes, let's," she agreed. "I'm starving, and I'll take this up with blabbermouth Babby tomorrow." She chuckled.

"Go easy on her, she just wanted you to have a nice dinner." Raymond's eyes sparkled.

"Uh-huh. She wanted to play matchmaker and you know it." Laney elbowed him in the ribs, and he pretended to be wounded.

"Such grave accusations against an innocent lady." Raymond tried unsuccessfully to keep a straight face. "Ready?" he asked, opening the passenger door of his sleek sedan.

"Do I look okay?" Laney asked, doing a little twirl on the curb that made her dress float around her knees. "I don't seem to get out much anymore."

"Absolutely perfect," he assured her. The look in his eyes made Laney blush and she averted her gaze.

"You're too kind," she murmured, easing into the car, glad that the darkness hid the fire in her cheeks.

When they arrived at La Plage, Laney found herself still preoccupied with thoughts of the Evelyn Mattis case. There were so many questions that came up as she'd been digging. Where was Evelyn going? Why was the investigation closed so soon? What were the homicide detectives doing with the new evidence? She had to be careful not to let anything slip, since she had assured Detective Worth and Raymond that she'd leave well enough alone.

Laney made a concerted effort to bring herself back to the present, determined to enjoy a wonderful birthday dinner at the newest French restaurant in Shelburne. Everything from the amuse bouche to the aperitif was utterly spectacular, as was the wine that accompanied each course and just when Laney thought the lovely evening was coming to an end, the wait-staff came out with a small chocolate mousse layer cake, complete with candles, and sang Happy Birthday in French.

Though Laney was a bit self-conscious when her fellow diners glanced over at her table, she blew out her candles and smiled at the polite applause. She looked over at Raymond, and the look on his face, before a polite mask slipped over his features once again, made her pulse accelerate. She wanted to blame the glow that she felt in her midsection on the wine but had to admit to herself that it might just have something to do with Raymond Andrews. Which meant that he was dangerous, and she might need to make herself scarce for a bit…no matter how adorable those dimples might be. The dessert was every bit as good as the meal had been, and it paired well with the champagne that Raymond had ordered for the celebration.

"Thank you." Laney smiled at Raymond as the waiter took away the now-empty dessert plate. "This was perfect."

"You're very welcome," he replied. "I wanted to do something different – so I'm glad you liked it." He stood up. "Shall we?"

They rode back to Marcy's Tea Room in silence, but it wasn't an uncomfortable silence. Laney was pleasantly full, and the champagne had ensured that she felt nice and warm from head to toe, despite the cold weather. Raymond walked her to the front door of the Tea Room, pointedly ignoring her protests, and briefly squeezed her hand before saying goodnight. As she climbed into bed and burrowed under the covers, Laney smiled, and was asleep almost before her head hit the pillow.

"Happy Birthday, Laney-girl! And oh my goodness, can you believe it?!" Babby exclaimed the next morning, over a cup of Earl Grey tea and a blueberry muffin. Laney affected a surprised expression as Babby recounted the news article she had read about the cold case.

"They had to close down the trails right after you and Raymond got back because some hikers found evidence linked to this case of a missing woman from 1992," the older woman breathed, eyes wide.

"Wow…I guess we left just in time…" Laney replied, looking down at her hands.

"You knew all of this already, didn't you?" Babby arched an eyebrow at Laney. She put down her teacup and used her hand to lift Laney's chin so that she had no choice but to make eye contact. "Spill it."

Laney was oddly kind of relieved that now she finally had a reason to stop concealing the truth, so she told Babby everything about what had really happened on her weekend getaway. When she got to the part about Detective Worth, Babby interrupted.

"Wait, isn't that the lady who led the murder investigation for Mayor Andrews?"

"Yep, that's her." Laney nodded.

"Well, well, well." Babby pursed her lips. "I wonder if she's going to come back to Iberden for this case. You know the woman who went missing all those years ago was from here."

Laney admitted that she had done a little research on the case, but Babby interrupted again. "I was here when poor Evelyn went missing. That investigation dragged on for months before it finally stopped appearing in the news. They never found any clue as to where she might be, but they also didn't find evidence that she died, which I thought was odd at the time. I mean, it's such a small town, you'd think that someone would've known something."

Laney didn't want to pry, but when she saw the older woman's lower lip tremble a bit, she sensed that Babby was more connected to this case than she was letting on.

"You okay, Babby?" she asked softly.

"Evelyn was like a daughter to me," Babby whispered. "I always hoped she had just run away, that she was safe, but now..." Babby hesitated and sniffled. "I just wish I knew what happened. To have some closure, you know?"

Laney placed her hand over Babby's and suddenly the older woman raised her head, a fierce glint in her eyes.

"The end of the article said something about the case not being a top priority for the detective now since it's been cold for so long. I want to do some digging of my own," she proclaimed, her jaw set.

Laney was taken aback but completely on board. "What do you have in mind?"

"You remember Mayor Andrews' old neighbor, Larry Henderson?"

"The guy who was fighting with the mayor about moving his mailbox a while back?"

"That's the one," Babby confirmed. "He was also very interested in this case back in the day. I think it's time that I officially introduce you two. We'll just pay him a nice, friendly visit."

Laney knew where this was going, and although she felt like she should advise Babby against it, in the end she agreed to accompany her over to Mr. Henderson's house that afternoon. After all, what harm would it do? If the detective wasn't focusing on the case because it was old, then she and Babby wouldn't be interfering, and if they solved the case, Worth couldn't be upset, because it would be one less thing on her plate. That was her story, and she was sticking to it...for now at least.

CHAPTER FIVE

"Are you sure he won't mind us stopping by like this?" Laney shifted from one foot to the other after Babby rang Larry Henderson's doorbell. Her breath made puffy white clouds in the chilly air.

"Larry's lived in Iberden even longer than I have. He knows me well enough to accept when I randomly stop by." Babby shrugged. "Especially when I bring freshly-baked cookies."

Before Laney could argue, the front door opened and a tall, skinny, elderly gentleman stared down at them. He had a full head of long, silver hair and wore khaki pants with a black pullover sweater. Laney couldn't read the look on his face – the man looked as though he had been carved from stone.

But when he spotted the tray of still-warm chocolate chip cookies that Babby was holding, the corners of his lips curled up slightly.

Babby held out the tray. "Nice to see you Larry. I hope you're hungry - I made way too many of these to eat myself."

"You know I have a sweet tooth," he spoke in a gravelly voice. "They will certainly not go to waste." He turned his hawk-like gaze to Laney. "And you must be Miss Powers," he said stiffly. "Nice to officially meet you."

The cold formality of his tone was off-putting and made the hairs on the back of Laney's neck stand up a bit, but this man might have information that she and Babby needed, so she swallowed her discomfort and smiled.

"Please, call me Laney. I can't believe it's taken us this long to meet face-to-face. You'd think in a small town like Iberden, we'd already be great friends," she said lightly.

"I keep to myself most of the time." Larry gestured for the women to come inside. "Would you like a cup of coffee?" he offered, as they seated themselves in his immaculate dining room. "Of course, you probably prefer tea, don't you Laney, seeing as you run old Marcy's Tea Room now?" he asked sourly. "I swear, this town is stuck in the past. I mean really...a Tea Room? What is this, the Victorian era? Why don't we just have coffee houses on every corner like the rest of the country?"

Laney was astonished at the older man's rudeness, but again bit back the retort that rose to her lips in the interest of securing whatever information that Babby thought he might have.

"I can have tea whenever I want it, so a coffee would be a nice change, thank you." She gave Larry a look that dared him to challenge her.

"Make that two," Babby chimed in with a nervous laugh.

Larry returned Laney's steely gaze and opened his mouth as if he was going to say something else but then apparently thought better of it and placed the tray of cookies on the table. "Coming right up," he said, turning to the kitchen. "Just made a pot for me before you called, Babby. Perfect timing, really."

He sounded much more cheerful when he spoke to Babby, and when he came back into the dining room with three mugs on a tray, it was like he'd never been sour. Laney's guard was up, and though she was polite, she'd be keeping an eye on Larry Henderson.

"So." He sipped his coffee, then placed it on a coaster made of cork. "What *really* brings you two over here? And don't give me any more of this bologna about wanting me to meet Laney," he grumbled. "I know you, Babby. Every time you come by here with your cookies, you end up asking me for something, so let's cut to the chase, shall we?"

Laney gritted her teeth and sipped her coffee to keep from saying the things that came to mind in the face of Larry's abrupt manner.

"Okay, okay." Babby held up her hands in mock surrender. "I read something in the paper today about a story from back in the nineties and I thought you might be able to help us out with filling in the details." She paused, then smirked. "Seeing as we're the two oldest people in this town, I figured I'd ask you first. There, happy?"

Larry crossed his arms over his chest. "What kind of story are we talking about?"

"I'm talking about the missing girl from Iberden. Evelyn Mattis," Babby replied quietly, staring into her mug of coffee.

Larry closed his eyes as if trying desperately to recall the name, but Babby was having none of that. "My turn to call you out on your bologna," she said sharply. "I know you remember Evelyn and I know you were following that investigation like it was a prime-time TV show, back then." Her eyes narrowed as she glared at Larry, and Larry stared right back at her. Neither looked like they were going to budge an inch, so Laney decided to cut in.

"I was hiking near Centennial Woods this past weekend and accidentally uncovered some evidence from that case," she admitted.

Larry's face turned as white as one of the fancy damask napkins at Marcy's Tea Room, but he seemed to shake off his initial reaction pretty quickly and replaced his look of dismay with his now-familiar scowl.

"So, you're telling me," he said, looking right at Laney, "that you came to this town a few months ago and we have the first murder investigation in the history of Iberden, and now you somehow unearth evidence from a cold case, that was probably from before you were even out of high school? Well, isn't that just quite the coincidence." He turned to Babby. "She's a trouble-maker, this one." He pointed to Laney like she was a disobedient child.

Laney opened her mouth to speak, but Babby wisely beat her to it.

"Don't you go blaming any of this on Laney," she insisted. "I won't have it, Larry Henderson. All she did was inherit her grandma's place. This girl did everything she could to help the detective get to the bottom of that tragic event with the mayor. If anything, we should be thanking her."

Laney couldn't keep quiet anymore. She'd been raised to respect her elders, but this man's rudeness had pushed her over the edge. "I know that I somehow managed to get tangled up in a couple of messes since I arrived in Iberden, but all I want to do is to help Babby get some closure here, and I don't appreciate your tone. Can't you see that this poor woman is distraught? Can you really blame her for wanting to know what happened back then?" Laney placed her hand on Babby's as it rested on the table. "If you don't want to help us, that's just fine - we'll go, but if you can help and you don't...that's on you, Mr. Henderson. You live with that." Fuming, Laney stood up, but Babby remained in her seat, tears filling her eyes as she stared at Larry.

"Please, Larry," Babby whispered. "I was so upset back then - I couldn't even follow the investigation myself. I just wanted to know what you remembered."

Looking as though he had swallowed a lemon and shooting a glare in Laney's direction before turning to Babby, Larry spoke.

"Oh alright," he muttered, finally, pushing back his chair. "Come with me."

Larry led them through the kitchen, toward a staircase that led to the basement. Laney hesitated, unsure as to whether or not she wanted to follow this surly fellow below ground, but when she saw the look of relief on Babby's face, she trudged obediently along behind them. She had no idea what she might encounter but trusted that Babby knew what she was doing.

CHAPTER SIX

Larry switched on the basement light and the three of them made their way down the stairs. Laney reached back to close the door but before it completely clicked shut, Larry barked up at her. "Leave it open. It gets stuffy down here."

By the time she reached the bottom step, muttering to herself about some people's manners, Babby and Larry were already huddled over a desk in the corner, that was covered with newspaper clippings. Laney paused for a moment to take in her surroundings, which she had to admit, took her by surprise.

The basement looked like a detective's office. From the tall filing cabinets to the minimalist office furniture, and the immaculate floors, Larry had created quite the workspace. But what really caught Laney's attention was the far back wall. It was painted bright white and featured a time-line, ranging from 1940 to 2000. When she stepped closer, she realized that the time-line was filled with notes and stories about Iberden. Hard news, lifestyle articles, human interest pieces, and even handwritten letters, were tacked to the wall in specific places on the time-line.

Considering why they were there, Laney immediately turned her attention to 1992, searching for anything about Evelyn Mattis's disappearance. It would have been easy to miss, in and amongst all of the random pieces of paper, but Laney noticed a bright yellow post-it note labeled 'Mattis' after searching for about thirty seconds.

Curious as to what could possibly be revealed by a tiny post-it note, she looked closer and saw that the line underneath the name said, "Files 3-8."

"Hey! Get over here," Larry called out. He was still over by the desk with Babby but was holding up a file folder. "I've got what you're lookin' for if you'd just pay attention and stop wandering around. "

Supremely curious, Laney flushed with anger, but tamped it down – remembering her mission - and hurried over. Larry opened the folder in his hands and started to pass papers to Laney, who accepted them, though she wasn't sure if she was supposed to start reading yet. She hesitated after he handed her the fifth sheet, but Larry looked at her expectantly and finally Babby spoke.

"Read them."

Larry turned and walked away, while Babby sprang to her feet to hover over her shoulder as she sat down in a chair across the desk from Larry and began to read.

The first page was an article from June 13, 1992. Laney had already come across it in her initial search. It had a picture of Evelyn Mattis in the center, which Laney studied a little longer now. The young woman's carefree smile and wavy hair made it look like she was posing for the cover of a magazine.

The next page was a typed list of five names with notes beside them, though four of the names were crossed out. Laney glanced curiously at Babby, who seemed to understand her silent question.

"List of suspects," she said. "Larry gathered the list based on the police investigation and followed the news to see who was in the clear." She pointed at number four, the only one that wasn't crossed out. "That was the only one that didn't have a solid alibi, but I guess the cops couldn't get enough evidence to charge him."

Laney reread the name. *Arty Dale.* She knew the last name sounded familiar, but she couldn't place it until Babby spoke up, "That was the head park ranger who helped search the area where Evelyn was last spotted. You read the part about her planning a road trip, right?"

Laney nodded. "When her roommate came back to their apartment a few days after she went missing, she told the detectives that Evelyn mentioned planning a big road trip to Maine to see her cousins. But the roommate also said Evelyn hadn't solidified the plans when they last spoke."

Laney didn't remember reading anything about how Evelyn was last spotted in the park, though. She flipped through the last of the papers and found an article that she hadn't come across in her own research. It was dated June 27, 1992 - exactly two weeks after the original story. There were no pictures, and the first part of the article was just a recap of what she already knew, but when she got to the second half of the page, there was new information.

Evelyn Mattis's new credit card statement revealed several charges at the businesses near Centennial Woods. Her roommate confirmed that Evelyn mentioned that she wanted to stop in the area on her way to her cousins', but Evelyn hadn't planned to leave for at least another week. Her employer, Babette Olfas, of Babby's Antiques, confirmed that Evelyn had in fact requested two weeks off at the end of the month...

Wrapped up in the article, Laney had forgotten that Babby was reading over her shoulder until she heard her friend sniffle then walk away. She dropped the papers on the desk and approached the grieving woman, who was staring blankly at the timeline on the wall.

"I can't believe I didn't ask her what her plans were for the time off. If I had, maybe I would have been able to be more helpful in the investigation," she muttered shaking her head. "Instead, I was just 'the employer' who had no valuable information." Babby took a deep breath, squared her shoulders, and turned to face Laney. "I had most of the public information already, but what I didn't have was Larry's insight."

As if on cue, the dour, silver-haired man approached.

"So, I guess you wanna know why the park ranger wasn't cleared, right?" he asked, though he didn't wait for a response.

Instead, he handed them a file labeled *Dale*. It wasn't thick - probably only about ten sheets of paper, but Laney had a feeling that whatever was in the folder just might include some information that hadn't been released in the newspaper.

"How is it that you happen to have all of this information, Larry?" she asked. If he could be rudely straightforward, so could she.

"I'm a problem solver. Always have been, ever since I was a kid." He shrugged, not seeming the least bit put out by her question. "When I got older, I started following all kinds of different cases - not just ones in Iberden. I liked the challenge of trying to figure out the detectives' line of thinking. I tried to come to conclusions based on the evidence. You could call it hobby, I guess. Sometimes I even pitched my theories to the cops. Served as a deputy for a bit and helped out on a lot of cases. Babby knew about it," he added. "That's why she brought you here, I suppose."

Babby nodded vigorously. "Oh yes," she said. "I knew Larry was always on top of the news back then, but I do wonder why you stopped with it? It was around fifteen years ago, right?"

Larry looked oddly forlorn and absently ran his hand through his hair.

"I just realized that I needed to focus on my career," he mumbled. "I was a full time accountant and a volunteer deputy for forty years. I gave up on this silly hobby when I was up for partner at the firm. Don't know if it was worth it in the end, though. That job was sucking the life out of me. Eighty-hour work weeks more often than not, and the stress from the clients was brutal."

Nodding politely, Laney brought the conversation back to the matter at hand. "Well, we're glad you held onto all this stuff." She gestured to the timeline, then she held up the mysterious file of Ranger Dale. "Do you think we can take a look at some of this before we go?"

"Take it." Larry waved a hand. "I know everything that's in there. Unfortunately, none of it changes the fact that no one could prove the guy did anything wrong, but if you two wanna go down that rabbit hole, be my guest."

Laney and Babby exchanged a look and headed for the stairs, with Laney safeguarding the file folder under her arm. They both had one thing on their mind, get out of Larry Henderson's house before he changed his mind about letting them take the file.

CHAPTER SEVEN

Laney opened the front door of Marcy's Tea Room, ready to greet the early-risers of Iberden, and noticed the rolled up paper on the porch, which was strange for a Wednesday. She typically only received the Sunday paper. When she bent down to pick it up, she was surprised to discover that it wasn't her usual Iberden Chronicle.

Today's Truth was printed in bold across the single page that was rolled up and taped closed. Laney hurried back inside, broke the piece of tape, flattened the sheet of paper against the nearest table, and began to read.

Good morning, Iberden, and welcome to the first edition of Today's Truth, your source for local news. I know what you're all thinking - Iberden is an open book. Everyone knows everyone else's business; there are no secrets, right? Wrong. I'm writing to make sure you're all aware of what's happening in the area. Today, there is breaking news related to an investigation that began right here in 1992.

Laney's jaw dropped. Easing into a chair, and hoping to finish before any customers came in, she continued reading.

On June 13, 1992, Evelyn Mattis, a young woman from Iberden, didn't show up for her shift at Babby's Antiques. The next day, after Evelyn missed another shift, her employer reported her missing. Authorities eventually called off the search without ever solving the case.

But, as of this past weekend, new evidence has been uncovered suggesting that the mysterious disappearance of the Iberden woman was actually a murder. Stay tuned for more updates on this disturbing turn of events.

Laney continued to stare at the page even after she read the last line. While there was always gossip in a small town, she never expected someone to go entirely off the rails like this. Who could have done such a thing? Considering that only she, Babby, Raymond, and Larry knew about the new developments in the case as of yesterday, it seemed that the most likely culprit would be Larry. It was also entirely possible that the older gentleman had simply let some of the information slip to someone else in town, who then took it upon themselves to spread the word. But who would Larry even tell? From what Laney had gathered after her visit with the somewhat surly senior citizen, he was a bit of a loner - and even he had said that he usually kept to himself...

She shook her head, as if that would clear the questions that were developing by the second. She wondered, with dismay, whether or not Babby had seen the strange little newspaper yet. The story had mentioned Babby's Antiques by name and Laney couldn't imagine that her friend would want this set of circumstances to be the talk of the town right now - she was already upset about the dark reminder of the loss of Evelyn. Biting her lip, Laney considered her options. She could find Babby before the older woman had a chance to discover the paper herself or she could track down Larry and figure out if he had something to do with the strange little article. In the end, she felt it was more important to find Babby. They could confront Larry together after she made sure that her tenderhearted friend was okay.

Laney grabbed the pot-stirring gossip column, rolled it back up, and headed out the front door in search of Babby, already pulling out her phone to call her. She was halfway out the door, pulling it shut behind her, when she was startled by a dearly familiar voice.

"Laney!" Babby called from the driveway beside the house. "Did you see it? Did you see it?" She held Today's Truth up, pain and disgust twisting her usually placid features. Laney sighed, wishing that she'd gotten to Babby sooner. She trotted quickly down the porch steps and met Babby between the sidewalk and the driveway, embracing her in a hug that she knew would convey all the words she couldn't say. Babby sobbed into her shoulder.

"This isn't right," Babby moaned. "What this paper did isn't going to help the case or bring honor to Evelyn's memory. This shouldn't have happened. Not to mention the fact that now I'm going to have the whole town looking at me like I'm the main attraction at a circus." She paused, then pulled back from the hug and wiped her eyes with the back of her hand. "Everyone in town has seen it and now they're all asking about what happened with Evelyn. Obviously, if I knew what had happened to her, the case would've been solved twenty-five years ago." She shook her head and pulled a tissue out of her pocket to dab at her nose, while Laney shivered in her thin white blouse. "Honestly, some of these folks act like *I'm* involved in her murder or something." She paused for a moment, her mouth working.

Laney could tell Babby was overwhelmed, but she didn't know what to do to help. Figuring that her best option was to get the emotionally overwrought woman engaged in something other than the gossip rag that had the town buzzing, Laney said what she thought would either be the worst possible or best possible thing to say, under the circumstances. "I think Larry's behind it."

Babby's blinked twice, taking in the statement, and her brows rose. "I trusted him with this information," she said softly. "If he went behind my back and started telling the town about this..." Her mouth clamped shut and her lips compressed into a thin line.

Laney placed her hand on the Babby's shoulder. "You wanted closure, right?"

Babby nodded, seemingly lost in thought. "Yes I do, let's get to the bottom of this." There was a determined glint in her eyes. "We'll figure out who's leaking information about the case and maybe we'll even get a step closer to finding out what happened to Evelyn. We'll start with Larry," she said firmly. "But we need to do some research on our own first - we'll confront him when we have some better information to hold over his head."

Laney wondered whether they were both acting rashly, but when she saw the spark return to Babby's eyes, she knew that, at least for the moment, they were making the right decision. "I think you're absolutely right, Babby. Meet me back here at the Tea Room at noon and we can get started. I'll make arrangements for Carly to stay a little later in case I need her to close."

"Then I'll see you at noon." Babby moved back toward her car. Her shoulders were no longer slumped in defeat. She had her fire back and was a woman on a mission once more.

CHAPTER EIGHT

Laney heard her phone vibrate on the desktop where she and Babby huddled together in front of her laptop, peering at the screen. Neither of them felt compelled to turn their attention away from what they were reading, so the phone continued to vibrate, the buzzing noise filling the otherwise silent room.

"Are you going to answer that?" Babby's eyebrows rose.

"Ughhh," Laney groaned.

She pushed back her chair and stood up to lean over and check the phone screen to see who was interrupting their sleuthing. Oddly, when she saw

Raymond's name flash across the screen, she couldn't help but feel a bit uneasy and wondered what he might think when he found out what she and Babby were up to. Had he seen Today's Truth? Lost in thought, she hesitated just long enough to let the call go to voicemail.

"Who was it?" Babby asked, looking at her oddly.

"Raymond." Laney paused, then looked up to find Babby staring at her. "I'll call him back later."

She tried to keep her voice casual, and was relieved when Babby shrugged, then turned her attention back to their research. Laney turned the phone face down, hoping the old saying 'out of sight, out of mind' would apply to her guilt. She and Raymond had promised Detective Worth to stay out of the investigation, and Laney was quite certain that Raymond was holding up his end of the bargain, even though she wasn't. When she returned to her chair, Laney was immediately drawn to what was currently displayed on the screen. Her mouth dropped open in a little O of surprise. "Is that...?"

"Yup." Babby nodded.

The picture was clear - same tall and skinny build; same thick hair that Laney noticed yesterday. "Larry," she murmured. "But why is he dressed in a sheriff's uniform?"

"According to the article," Babby said, squinting at the fine print, "Larry Henderson was the next in line for sheriff back in 1989 - right before I moved here. Seems like he was passed up for some other guy. Look at this guy," she pointed. "He looks kind of familiar, doesn't he?"

Laney nodded slowly, remembering the friendly man who had helped her through the murder investigation a few months ago, Bill. "I'd bet anything that guy is related to Sheriff Bill," Laney mused.

Babby's eyes lit up. "Yes," she exclaimed. "I wonder if that was his grandfather?" She used her pointer finger to scan down the article until she reached the end. "This article is from the nineties, so it wouldn't mention Bill, but I think you're right, here's the name - Mark Howard...well that seems a bit too much to be just a coincidence. He has Sheriff Bill's last name, for Pete's sake." She closed the current window and did a quick search. As soon as the results popped up,

Laney and Babby saw the list of family members and stopped when they reached 'Bill Howard.'

"Guess that explains why Larry was never reconsidered for sheriff- the position seems to run in the family," Laney observed dryly.

"But." Babby shook a finger at her. "It doesn't tell us what happened back then that made them choose Mark Howard over Larry. You see here?" She clicked back to the original news story. "The sheriff before Mark didn't have the same last name, which means they probably decided against Larry for a reason. It wasn't a Howard family dynasty yet." Babby frowned. "Seems like a strange coincidence that the case was investigated a few years after Larry missed his chance at being sheriff and yet he was still so involved…maybe even obsessed…"

Laney knew what her friend was implying, but she didn't want to jump to any conclusions. "We'll have to dig into it more to find out if this is a real lead." She had barely finished her sentence when Babby cleared her throat and pointed at the new page on the computer screen.

Laney scooted her chair a little closer and began to read the article from July of 1989, titled "Race for the

Sheriff of Iberden Comes to an End." Laney carefully read each word and didn't look away from the screen until the very end, which was when she turned to Babby, wide-eyed. "Larry interfered with another missing person investigation?" she whispered.

"Sure looks that way," Babby agreed. "Now can we agree we have a reason to suspect him?" She stood up and put her hands on her hips, tapping her foot.

Laney sighed. "I mean, I'll agree with you that it doesn't look good." She paused and flipped her braid over her shoulder. "But talking to Larry and getting his help was your idea in the first place, remember?"

"Yes, but that was before we knew the whole story."

"We still don't know the whole story," Laney pointed out, but Babby had already moved on.

"Now that we know that Larry got in trouble before for butting in where he didn't belong, who's to say he didn't do it again?" Babby challenged.

"Then why wasn't he a suspect in Evelyn's case back then?" Laney shot back. "If what he did was so bad, don't you think the police would've looked into Larry more as a suspect?"

"I guess we're going to have to find out now, aren't we?" Babby folded her arms.

The doorbell rang, interrupting the conversation, and Babby followed Laney downstairs when she went to see who was there. Laney was surprised when she opened the door and saw Raymond standing on her porch, looking flustered, worried even.

"I called," he said. "And texted."

Laney stood back so that he could come in out of the cold and thanked her lucky stars that she hadn't brought her phone to the door with her. "Oh no, I hope you weren't worried. The battery in my phone must have died." She shrugged, feeling the weight of Babby's gaze on her as she fibbed to Raymond. "What's up?"

Raymond gave her a measured look but didn't press the matter further. "Did you get the paper today?"

"Yes I did. I was absolutely shocked when I saw it on the porch this morning." That at least was truthful.

"The Sheriff called me today about it. For some reason, he thought I might have an idea of who was behind it, but I told him I didn't know anything about the case." He looked at Babby, who was studying her fingernails. "Babby?" he said. "I assume Laney told you about what we found on our trip?"

Babby chuckled. "I think you're busted, Laney."

Laney shrugged and nodded, looking sheepish. "I know that we told Detective Worth that we wouldn't say anything, but Babby has a personal interest in this case."

"You *really* believed that I thought you wouldn't tell anyone about the hike?" He smiled. "Laney, I knew you wouldn't be able to keep this from Babby for long. I'm actually a little surprised that you didn't tell her until today."

"She's known for a while now, actually," Laney confessed, not remorseful in the least.

Raymond crossed his arms and looked from Laney to Babby and back again. "Alright, I feel like you two know more about this than I do, so why don't you fill me in?"

Babby headed for the door. "Actually, I have someplace that I need to be, so you bring Raymond up to speed, Laney." Babby exited with a quick wave before she closed the door behind her.

"Gee, thanks," Laney muttered under her breath, glaring at her friend for abandoning her as she scooted out the door. "Let's see...where do I begin?"

CHAPTER NINE

After yesterday's conversation with Raymond, Laney felt at least a bit better about the Evelyn Mattis case. While he was rightfully concerned that she and Babby were taking on something that was complicated and potentially dangerous, when Laney explained the circumstances, he had to agree that Laney had done the right thing by offering to help her friend. She reviewed what they had talked about after Babby left the Tea Room.

"Honestly, if I were in your position, I probably would have done the same thing. "Raymond confessed, still looking worried. Laney knew that there would be a 'but' coming soon, so she wasn't surprised by Raymond's next sentence.

"But since I'm the Mayor of Iberden now, it wouldn't exactly be prudent for me to interfere with an ongoing investigation."

Torn between wanting to help Babby and wanting to insulate Raymond from any consequences that might arise from being involved, Laney suggested the only thing she could think of.

"What if I don't tell you anything else about what Babby and I may or may not be doing from here on out?" she suggested. "That way, Babby and I can continue…doing whatever it is that we may or may not be doing, without dragging you any further into the whole mess."

Raymond looked skeptical, but Laney didn't give him a chance to interrupt.

"I'm not telling you to lie about what you know," she insisted. "You can even go tell the sheriff everything that we've uncovered so far. We didn't do anything wrong…yet. But for your sake, let's not discuss the case from here on out. Okay?"

Raymond still didn't look entirely convinced, but Laney could tell that he understood where she was coming from. She could almost see the pro and con list being created in his head as the seconds passed. She didn't want to rush him, so she pulled her phone out of her pocket and started scrolling like she didn't have a care in the world. Raymond gave her a pointed look and nodded at the phone.

"Thought your battery was dead." He cocked an eyebrow at her.

Laney could feel the color rising in her cheeks.

"It must've just been resting." She gave him a dazzling smile and shrugged. "So, what do you think?"

Raymond stared at her for a few seconds, then finally shook his head.

"I guess that's the best option," he said, sounding reluctant. "I can't ask you to not help Babby just because it might look bad for me. But you're right, if I don't know the details, then I'm not doing anything unethical - at least not technically…"

"Exactly!" Laney smiled triumphantly.

"Just be careful," Raymond warned. "I know everything turned out fine with my dad's case, but even that could have ended badly for you. When you're investigating something as serious as a potential murder, you may get more trouble than you bargained for, Laney."

"I know, I know." She waved a hand, dismissing his concerns. "We'll be careful." She rationalized that everything would be fine. She and Babby were going to be talking to Larry Henderson, for crying out loud. The man was practically elderly and had been an accountant – how dangerous could he be?

Once she'd shooed Raymond out the door with promises to be careful, Laney decided to take a break from murder and intrigue for an evening, and spent her time on the couch, watching TV and eating Chinese food that she ordered in. It was a welcome respite that she knew she'd need before taking on an investigation with Babby in the morning.

Laney filled Babby in on the way things were going to work going forward and the two of them marched through the door of the sheriff's station, filled with determination, right around noon, the next day. Laney knew that Raymond had talked to Bill earlier that morning about things, so she figured the sheriff would be expecting her and Babby to start asking questions soon anyway.

Apparently, Mr. Dale had been the head of the park service in that area for the past twenty-five years, so he had actually been heavily involved in the search for Evelyn when she went missing. Nothing referencing any kind of suspicion toward him had been released officially in the news at the time, but Larry's file did have some notes that piqued Laney's interest. There was documentation which showed that the entire department at the Centennial Woods park service location had to go through a year of training shortly after Evelyn's case was dropped. Laney wondered about what could have happened during that search to have prompted such an action.

When she had initially spoken with Detective Worth and Mr. Dale, they both mentioned that the park service was significantly understaffed at the time, but they also seemed to drop the subject pretty quickly. After Babby and Laney reviewed all of their research to date, they confirmed that not a single article mentioned this detail, which made them even more curious about the extent of the problem.

Babby was still firmly convinced Larry was the guy to watch, but Laney didn't want to jump to conclusions without doing all their homework, which is how she found herself waiting outside Sheriff Bill's office while Babby settled herself in the reception area. It had been Babby's suggestion that it might be best to only have one of them ask the sheriff questions, and it made sense that Laney should be the one to do it, since word had spread that she and Raymond happened to be hiking at Centennial Woods right before the first issue of Today's Truth had appeared. In fact, Laney had that day's copy of the gossip column tucked in her coat pocket, ready to refer to it during her little chat with the sheriff.

She knocked twice on the sheriff's door and in no time at all Bill was holding it open and waving Laney inside with a warm smile, like they were just about to have an ordinary conversation that had nothing to do with suspects and murder in the small town of Iberden.

"Please, sit," he invited, returning to his side of the desk. Laney took the seat across from him and placed her handbag on the floor beside her chair. When she sat back up, she noticed a steaming mug in front of her.

"I made coffee," Bill explained. "I figured if we're going to have a talk about all the hoopla going on around here these days, we might as well enjoy a cup of coffee too."

He picked up his own cup and took a long sip.

"So, the mayor - I mean Raymond - stopped by today and had some interesting things to say regarding you, Babby Olfas, and the investigation of the Mattis cold case."

He drummed his fingers against the edge of the desk and raised his eyebrows. "Now that it's out in the open, why don't you tell me why you're here today? I presume this is related to the case?"

Rather than respond directly, Laney leaned over and dug the most recent copy of Today's Truth out of her purse, placing it on the desk between them. She pointed at the headline. *"Cold Case is Heating up in Iberden."*

It was obvious by the look on his face that Bill had already seen the article.

"Babby and I are not taking the investigation into our own hands, if that's what you're thinking." She paused, waiting for him to reply, but he said nothing.

"And we have nothing to do with this ridiculous gossip column. Now that I think about it though, it does seem a bit strange that our regular newspaper isn't posting any details about the status of the investigation, particularly since there are probably plenty of people in town who were here when Evelyn went missing."

Bill grimaced. "Are you suggesting that I am not aware of Babby's and Larry Henderson's connection to this case?"

The question hung in the air between them. Laney figured that it was rhetorical and stayed silent, waiting for him to continue.

"You may think that you know more about this case than I do, Miss Powers, but I can assure you that I am well-informed and am being more than cooperative with the detectives who are looking into everything related to Evelyn's case. At this point, we don't even know with any degree of certainty whether the remains that were discovered are connected to that case or not."

Laney's mouth fell open. "I found human bones – who else could they possibly belong to?"

"They have not yet officially been identified as belonging to Evelyn Mattis. We're not trying to hide information - we just want to make sure we have all the facts before we make a statement."

In her zealous quest for the truth, Laney hadn't considered that, and now that she took the time to listen to Bill's side of things, she felt more than a bit foolish. Though she had originally come to see the sheriff so that she could wheedle information from him about the old park ranger and Larry, she decided not to continue with her plan.

"I'm sorry, Sheriff. I completely understand. I never meant to imply that you and the detectives weren't doing your jobs. I just hoped that maybe there could finally be some closure surrounding this case, and I might have jumped the gun a bit," Laney confessed, feeling the heat in her cheeks.

"You're nothing if not persistent." Sheriff Bill chuckled and stood, offering his hand.

Laney shook it and beat a hasty retreat. When she reached the reception area, Babby was nowhere to be found. Laney sighed and wondered if she'd been duped. Had Babby known that talking to the sheriff would be a fool's errand? Had the whole plan been nothing more than a ruse to occupy Laney's time so that Babby could go meet with Larry on her own? Laney couldn't be sure, but she knew darn well what she had to do in order to find out.

CHAPTER TEN

Laney felt her phone vibrating in her pocket and pulled it out right away, wondering if it was Babby. When she checked the caller ID and saw that it was Roger, her heart sank. She had entirely forgotten to call the man who was like an adopted grandfather to her.

"Hey, Roger," she answered cheerfully.

"Well, it's good to hear your voice, Laney," he replied, not sounding hurt at all, thankfully. "I'm not sure if Babby told you, but Janet and I are in town, and we wanted to catch up if you have some time."

"I'm so glad you called. Yes, she actually told me the other day, but we've just had a lot going on and I forgot to call. I'm so sorry," Laney apologized. She was still a bit preoccupied, wondering what mischief Babby might have gotten herself into when she disappeared from the police station, but she gave Roger her full attention.

"Oh, don't apologize, honey, it's no big deal," Roger assured her, his voice warm. "I was hoping that you might have some free time today for a cup of tea."

"Umm..." Laney wracked her brain trying to come up with a polite excuse to get out of the invitation but came up blank.

It wasn't that she didn't want to see Roger – she really enjoyed his company, and his presence reminded her of her beloved Grandma Marcy – it was just that his timing was about as bad as it could get. Roger seemed to mistake her silence as agreement.

"Does four o'clock work for you?" he asked. "I can just meet you at the Tea Room."

The hope in his voice tugged at Laney's heartstrings. She was torn. On one hand, she didn't want to do anything that would hurt Roger's feelings, on the other hand, there was no telling what shenanigans

Babby might indulge in if left to her own devices. Thinking fast, Laney figured, a bit overly optimistically, that if she hurried, she could track down Babby, talk some sense into her, and meet Roger at the Tea Room at four, without having to tell him about Evelyn Mattis. It was an ambitious plan, but she thought that she could manage it.

"Sure, Roger," she replied brightly. "Four o'clock is perfect. I'll see you then."

"I'm looking forward to it. We haven't talked in a while and I have some exciting news," Roger replied. Laney wasn't really paying attention to his last sentence and gave him a quick "I'm looking forward to it, too," before saying goodbye and hanging up.

Laney immediately tried to call Babby but her call went straight to voicemail so she decided to just head over to Larry's house, where she suspected that her well-meaning but naïve friend might already be conducting an interrogation. Hopefully, she wasn't unknowingly interviewing a murderer. Laney headed for the door, but froze in her tracks, wondering if she should give Raymond a call. Reinforcements might be nice…just in case.

Torn, and knowing that time was of the essence, she dismissed the idea, remembering that she had just promised Raymond that she wouldn't share any details of what she and Babby were doing. She briefly considered giving the sheriff a heads up, but also shut that idea down, since he had been less than supportive of their efforts. Besides, she didn't actually know that anything was wrong yet. As of right now, she just needed to keep her wits about her and stay calm until she had reason to panic. Babby could be doing something entirely harmless and innocent. Or she could be badgering a murderer, but Laney would never find out if she continued to stand in her foyer thinking about her options. With a determined lift of her chin, she hurried to the kitchen to let Carly know that she'd be gone for a bit, then she strode right out the door before she could change her mind or start overthinking again.

Laney walked boldly up the steps to Larry's front porch, her stomach feeling like a quivering bowl of Jello, and knocked on the door, before she could talk herself out of it. She could hear footsteps approaching, and a quick glance around didn't seem to indicate any sign of a disturbance. When Larry opened the door, his brows rose, as though he was surprised to see her, and he peeked over Laney's shoulder, as if he were searching for someone else.

"I didn't expect to see you, young lady." Larry seemed confused. "Did Babby forget something? I didn't notice that she had much with her besides her tote bag, but I could be wrong, I suppose."

Laney didn't want Larry to know that she had no idea what he was talking about, figuring that if she did, he might not give her the information she wanted. So, she tried to play it cool.

"No, not exactly," she replied. "Babby just called to tell me that she stopped by but her phone battery was about to die so she didn't get to explain everything." Laney improvised, refusing to feel guilty about the tiny fib. "I couldn't quite hear where she was headed, but I thought maybe she said she was going up to Centennial Woods, so I figured I'd just come over here and check before I headed all the way out there." She smiled expectantly, hoping that the old man wouldn't decide to become hostile toward her again.

Larry didn't even hesitate. "Oh, of course, I should have known that you would be meeting her up there for her little investigation." He paused, thinking. "I would have thought that she'd have told you about it in advance, but then again she does have a habit of coming up with ideas at the last second and jumping in with both feet." He chuckled, which was a bit disconcerting. Laney hadn't been sure that the man even knew how to smile.

Laney barked out a nervous laugh. "You know Babby," she replied. "When she gets one of her ideas, she doesn't wait for anyone…by the way, what exactly did she need from you before she drove up there?" She tried to make her voice sound as casual and nonchalant as possible, not wanting to spook the old guy, particularly if he was a murderer, a possibility that she couldn't discount, at present. "She didn't get to tell me what it was before the phone died, so I just want to make sure that I have all of the pertinent info when I meet her."

Laney held her breath, gazing innocently at Larry and trying to gauge his reaction.

He frowned. "I actually didn't have what she wanted. She asked for the park ranger's home address and phone number because she was going to reach out to him directly." He shrugged. "I told her she'd just have to find him over at one of the parks. She seemed a little annoyed, but that's her problem. What do I look like a phone book?"

"She just knows that you're a great source for information when she has an issue, I think," Laney replied, being intentionally diplomatic. "Well, I'd better get out there to see what she's up to." She edged away from the door, not wanting to seem like she was in too much of a hurry. "Thanks, Larry."

She was about to turn around and leave when she spotted something on Larry's hand...black smudges that looked alarmingly like...printer's ink. Larry saw her interest and glanced down at his hands.

"What are you looking at?" he asked, shoving his hands in his pockets.

"I just noticed that you had some smudges on your hands, that's all." Laney stared him down, too angry to be as scared as she should have been. "Got a printing press down in that basement of yours, Mr. Henderson?" she asked, eyes narrowed.

"What's it to you?"

"Babby and I came here and shared my discovery with you, in confidence. Why on earth would you go and act like the town crier, bringing everyone in on it?" Laney demanded.

"Maybe because this town needs to wake up. There's been way too much lazy policing done here, and they need to get their act together. If I had been made sheriff back in the day..." Larry broke off his sentence and clamped his mouth shut, then began again. "If you want your business kept quiet, then you need to learn how to keep your mouth shut, kid."

"Thanks for the words of wisdom. We trusted you. Clearly we shouldn't have," Laney shot back.

Something sparked in Larry's eyes. "Don't even think about trying to pin what happened to that girl on me," he threatened. "It won't go well for you, I promise you that."

With that, he slammed the door in Laney's face.

Her heart pounding like mad, Laney checked the time - 3:50 pm. Now she was in a quandary. As much as she didn't want to stand Roger up, with no explanation, there was no way in the world that she could be honest with him about what she was about to do. He was very protective and would almost certainly insist that Laney stay home and be safe, but it was too late for that. Who knew what Babby might be about to encounter? Laney was faced with either slipping away now, before Roger arrived at the Tea Room, or facing him and having to lie. As awful as standing him up would be, she couldn't bring herself to even think about lying to the sweet old man, even if it was for an important cause.

"I'll just text him that something came up," she murmured aloud, hurrying toward the Tea Room so that she could get in, tell Carly to close up at five, and get back out again without being seen by Roger. Her heart ached, but it was for the best right now. She'd just have to make it up to him later.

CHAPTER ELEVEN

The drive to The Evergreen Bed and Breakfast didn't take too terribly long, but Laney tried to spend the time in the car planning, rather than worrying about what was to come. She hadn't even bothered to call Babby again, figuring that her friend had set out on a one-woman mission, determined to get some information out of the potentially dangerous park ranger, though now Laney had her doubts about Larry as well. The Evergreen was the nicest place in the area to stay, and Laney would bet her bottom dollar that Babby had checked in recently.

The sign for The Evergreen came up on her left and Laney scanned the parking lot for Babby's car, a triumphant smile playing about her lips when she spotted the purple sedan. Given the scant number of cars in the lot, she should have no problem securing a room for the night...or for however long their investigation, which hopefully wouldn't turn into a wild goose chase, might take.

Laney pulled into a parking spot right next to Babby's, tossed her hastily-packed tote bag over her shoulder and marched inside. She'd been dreading having to try to figure out where Babby might be, but much to her surprise and relief, Laney found her friend sitting alone at a three person table in the main lobby, sipping a large cup of coffee. She was fully prepared to give Babby a nice long lecture about needing to plan things more carefully rather than dashing out on impulse, but as soon as Babby looked up and noticed her, the elderly woman's face fell with genuine disappointment. Laney was baffled and decided to hear Babby out before giving her a much-needed, but perhaps ill-timed lecture.

Trying to channel her inner Zen, Laney sat down across from Babby, but didn't say anything, keeping her expression neutral.

Twirling a strand of her short gray hair nervously, Babby appeared to be deciding where to start.

"We had a lead," she finally began, staring down at the table top. "Well, multiple leads and I wasn't about to waste valuable time by waiting around for all this nonsense with talking to the sheriff when I could be here making progress on the case." Her jaw jutted forward, and she crossed her arms in defiance. "I know you had a plan and I know you thought it was best, but we were wasting time," Babby insisted, her voice rising. Laney glanced around to see if anyone had witnessed the outburst, relaxing slightly when she determined that they were the only occupants. "I mean, I didn't know when you offered to help that you'd be taking over everything…and that we'd even have to care what Raymond or the sheriff thought." Babby lowered her voice, looking hurt.

Laney found herself wishing that she didn't have to face this particular little nugget of truth. Babby was right. Laney had been the one who decided what they would do and when they would do it up to this point, while Babby had faded helplessly into the background. It wasn't right. The whole point of getting involved was supposed to be about helping Babby get closure, but Laney had completely lost sight of that original goal after getting swept up into all of the details and potential dangers of the case.

As realization struck her with full force, she felt ashamed.

She gazed at her friend wordlessly for a moment, swallowing hard, then clearing her throat so that she could speak.

"Babby, you're right. I messed up and I'm sorry. Sometimes when what I want to do is help, I just end up taking charge, and that wasn't the right thing to do. This case isn't about me. It's about you and I'm sorry that for a little while, I forgot that."

"And it's about poor Evelyn," Babby said with a sad smile. "Apology accepted. I guess I owe you an apology too...I should have talked to you before I ran out here by myself."

"What's done is done." Laney shrugged. "Now, why don't you tell me the plan so I can help."

Babby pulled out the file on the park ranger that they had studied the other day and pointed to a specific line. "It says Mr. Dale was questioned by the police three times, and the last time was related to some charges on Evelyn's credit card around when she went missing. I find it very interesting that the day after he was questioned, the mandatory park ranger training went into effect"

"Sorry, Babby, I'm just not connecting the dots here...why do you feel like this is so important?" Laney frowned.

"We need to figure out how Dale is connected to those shops in town. I'd bet anything there's a link," Babby insisted. "And I'd bet my last dime that the park ranger training was just a cover for something else."

"Or maybe a smokescreen to make him look like he was doing everything that he could to be of help," Laney mused, trying to puzzle out any kind of pattern or connection between the disparate pieces of information that they had. "So, if that's the case, we need to talk to people at the places where Evelyn made purchases before she went missing, as well as talking to the park ranger. But what on earth are we going to say to Mr. Dale?"

"We tell him about the gossip column and maybe embellish it a little...make him think that someone is writing about him and his connection to the case," Babby explained. "We'll make him nervous so that he might just start poking into things himself, then we'll follow along and let him lead us right to the evidence."

Laney had quite a few doubts about the plan, but she bit her tongue, reminding herself that she was doing this for Babby. There was one concern, however, that needed to be voiced.

"I know that it's a bit late to be bringing this up, but don't you think it might be dangerous trying to tail a murder suspect on our own?" she asked.

"That's part of the reason I came here by myself," Babby admitted. "I figured this was my responsibility - or at least, it wasn't yours. You have your whole life ahead of you, and I...well, I've done most of my living. I've heard that people can accomplish great things when they don't have much to lose."

Laney reached out and grabbed Babby's hands before she replied. "We're in this together Babby, you have a lot of living left in front of you, and if you really wanna do this, I'm going to help. I'm assuming you have a plan for finding Dale?"

"One step ahead of you." Babby smirked. "According to the parks department, he's the head ranger at Centennial Woods East today, until 7 pm. I was planning to head over there around dinner time so maybe it would be quiet, and we could get a little time to talk to him."

Laney checked her phone. It was 5:15 pm. "Well, should we go find somewhere to eat before we head out there, then?"

"I was hoping you'd suggest that." Babby chuckled. "I'm starving."

Laney laughed, then stood and stretched before approaching the front desk, where the local takeout menus were on display. "Pizza, breakfast for dinner, or Mexican? You pick."

"Definitely breakfast for dinner," Babby replied. "I've been craving French toast since you told me about the breakfast you had here and now I won't have to wait until tomorrow morning."

CHAPTER TWELVE

Babby and Laney were seated in a large booth at the Burlington Diner, waiting for their food to be served and Babby recited her plan aloud once again, thinking through every step while they sipped piping hot coffee, warming their hands on the thick porcelain mugs.

"So, I'll introduce myself and then you'll remind Dale of who you are...I'm sure he'll remember you from last weekend, so that just makes things a little easier for us," she mused. "Then we'll make some small talk about the park and how much we enjoy hiking."

Laney nodded mechanically. They'd gone through all of this on the ride over, but she wanted to be supportive.

"Then we mention Today's Truth. We'll use that to try and get his attention, then we leave him hanging with the bait, that the latest issue was about him," Babby summed up and sighed. "Why is it that when I say it out loud, it all just sounds a little bit risky and ridiculous? You think he'll suspect anything?" she asked Laney, twisting her white paper napkin nervously.

"Hard to say, but I think it's definitely a good starting point," Laney answered truthfully.

She decided not to distract Babby with the news that she'd discovered the identity of the author of Today's Truth. Babby considered Larry a friend and Laney didn't feel like disillusioning her any further at the moment. Though she wasn't so sure about sneaking around after the park ranger, this first part of the plan seemed simple enough. Babby opened her mouth as if she were about to ask another question, but then her eyes lit up and focused on something behind Laney.

The server approached with the two heaping plates of good old fashioned home cooking.

"Cinnamon French toast?" she asked.

Babby eagerly raised her hand and reached for the plate. The server chuckled as she placed the plate carefully in front of Babby, then turned to Laney.

"And you ordered the omelet?"

"Yes, thank you." Laney smiled, as the server hurried away to see to a customer who was waving at her.

The place was packed. Nearly every table was filled and the soothing sound of cutlery striking porcelain mingled with the lackadaisical end-of-day chatter. Laney took the first bite of her sausage and cheddar omelet and closed her eyes, savoring the perfect balance of flavors. Her stomach growled audibly, and she had to exercise extreme discipline to keep from shoveling the delectable dish into her mouth. She looked up and saw that Babby was devouring her own dish, drenching the fluffy, perfectly-prepared French toast in a pool of warm maple syrup, and adding a slab of thick, creamy butter to the top of the stack for good measure.

Between bites, Babby continued her microanalysis of the plan. If Laney hadn't been so preoccupied with her food, she would've been mildly annoyed, though she would've tried to hide it.

"So," she continued, "if he's guilty, we have to make Dale feel like he has something to lose. Either he really does have something to cover up and we can just follow him, or he's innocent and we can cross him off the list."

Babby paused then shrugged. Laney nodded absently, focused on her dinner. She'd discovered that if she took a bite of the fluffy biscuit that had come with her omelet, before forking up a good-sized hunk of egg and sausage, it tasted like the world's most glorious breakfast sandwich.

"It's win-win in my book." Babby added a little more syrup to her plate. "Although I am kind of banking on this leading to something productive because we're running low on options," she admitted.

Laney nodded, having no idea what Babby had just said. They ended up finishing their food and leaving the busy diner just before six o'clock, and since they were merely minutes away from Centennial Woods East, they arrived at the park ranger's office right as

HOT TEA AND A COLD CASE

people were beginning to leave. So far the plan was working like clockwork. There was only one truck in the parking lot when they pulled in, and Laney suspected that red pickup most likely belonged to Mr. Dale, himself.

She had barely turned off the car and Babby had already unbuckled her seatbelt and was opening the door. She looked back at Laney impatiently. "Ready?" She raised her brows.

"Hold your horses." Laney smiled and shook her head.

Grabbing her purse and locking the car after she got out, she caught up with Babby by the front door of the park service office. The sign said that it was open until seven-thirty today, so the two women entered without having to knock or announce their arrival. Babby went in first, dragging Laney in behind her. Just as the door swung closed behind them, Laney saw a familiar face.

"Hello, ladies! How can I help you today?" Mr. Dale asked casually, tipping his hat to them in turn.

"Hello, sir." Babby gave him her warmest, most grandmotherly smile. "My name's Babby and this is my friend, Laney. We were actually looking for Park Ranger Dale."

He raised his eyebrows. "Well, you found him," he replied. "How can I be of service?"

Babby hesitated, then looked to Laney, who shrugged uncertainly.

"Well…" Babby faltered. "Do you have a few minutes to chat? We don't have a problem per se, but there is a bit of a concern that we wanted to discuss with you."

Laney could tell Babby was getting flustered already, so she cleared her throat and smoothly took over.

"Mr. Dale, I don't know if you remember me, but I'm the woman from this past weekend who came across some…unexpected findings on the trail around here?" She widened her eyes meaningfully, and the park ranger nodded.

"You're the woman from Iberden," he remembered. "You're acquainted with Detective Worth, if I recall." He chuckled and shook his head. "She told me you'd get involved in this, but I thought she was kidding."

Busted. Laney's heart skipped a beat. She hadn't even considered the fact that the park ranger might give the detective a call and rat them out for interfering. Yet again, her emotions had overcome her good sense, and she'd acted without considering the potential consequences.

"You know," Dale continued, "I don't really agree with Worth's stance on a lot of things anyway, so it doesn't matter a lick to me that she doesn't want you meddling. In fact, I find it kind of interesting that regular folks like you two just decided to throw caution to the wind and try to help. So, yeah, let's sit down, the three of us, and chat over a cup of coffee."

Dale took his keys out of his jacket pocket and spun them around once. "You ladies like the First Roaster?" he asked. When neither Babby nor Laney answered, he explained, "It's the best coffee shop in town. Right down the street. I would've thought that you'd heard of it."

"I could use a coffee." Laney nodded, and Babby followed suit.

Once they were seated at a round oak topped table in the tantalizingly aromatic coffee shop with their drinks, Babby got down to business.

"So, Mr. Dale," she began.

"Please," he interrupted, "call me Henry." He gave her a smile that seemed a bit patronizing, then sipped at his latte.

"Okay, Henry. We wanted to talk to you about the cold case that seems to be heating back up – you know, the one from the 90's, about the missing Iberden woman," she clarified.

"You brought a partner with you to investigate, Laney? Worth told you not to talk about the case as I recall…did you go and tell everyone?" He chuckled.

"No." Laney arched an eyebrow at him, baffled by his somewhat cavalier attitude toward such a serious topic. "I actually didn't have to start spreading the news. Someone else beat me to it." She took the first issue of Today's Truth out of her purse and set it on the table between them, smoothing the page with her hand.

Henry Dale stared at the paper before grabbing and skimming the front of the page. Laney and Babby watched silently as he read, until he finally put down the mysterious gossip column, ran his hand over his face, and sighed. "Has Detective Worth seen this?" he asked, seeming drained.

Laney and Babby both shrugged, and Laney realized that they hadn't really thought about that. Surely, someone in town would have brought it to Worth's attention.

"Our sheriff saw it, but we're not sure who else received a copy," Laney replied.

"We're thinking it just went out to Iberden," Babby added.

"She's going to flip out," the ranger muttered under his breath.

Laney had to agree. The detective already thought that Laney would try to get involved in the case. When she learned about the gossip rag, she'd blame Laney for sure. But that wasn't the point of this meeting. They had to stay focused on getting Henry to reveal something that could help them move forward. Judging by her next comment, Babby seemed to be on the same page.

"You know, Henry..." The older woman tapped on the table and gave the park ranger a sincere look. "Part of why we're showing you this is because a few issues have come out already and apparently, the investigators have decided to focus their efforts on prior suspects from back when Evelyn went missing..."

Giving Dale a meaningful look, she left the rest unsaid, but Henry clearly understood the implications.

"They're writing about me." He exhaled sharply and closed his eyes, as if deep in thought. When he opened them, Laney noticed what looked like a flash of anger in his expression.

"Well, are you two here to warn me about this heap of lies, or to accuse me of murder?" he asked quietly, eyes narrowed.

Laney felt the hair on the back of her neck rise in response to his tone and expression.

"We're not accusing you of anything, Mr. Dale," Babby assured him. "Honestly, we just want to get to the bottom of this and we thought you might be able to help us."

Laney wondered if Babby had changed their plan on the fly...again and was now planning to just tell the park ranger everything.

"We read that Evelyn had some charges on her credit card to a store out here and we were hoping you could tell us what store it was," she explained. "We think it can help us get to the bottom of this, and ultimately prove that you're innocent. "

Henry looked from Babby to Laney curiously. "Now, let me get this straight...You're saying you both came out here, against a directive from the police, to help me - some guy you don't even know - when you could just leave all this alone for the authorities to handle?" He paused, staring at each of them in turn. "Sorry ladies, I'm not buying it. There's more to the story here. Either tell me what's really going on or you can both be on your way." He looked at the door.

CHAPTER THIRTEEN

For whatever reasons of her own, Babby ended up telling Henry the truth. All of it. Apparently, she had decided that he seemed trustworthy, so she'd changed her plan and let the story out, come what may. Utterly bewildered, Laney had let her take the lead and hoped for the best. At least this way, if Dale was a killer, he'd think that he had them fooled and maybe they'd live to tell the tale. Maybe.

The upside was that this way they wouldn't have to sneak around trailing the ranger to see if he did anything suspicious, and once he heard all that they knew, he seemed to be on their side and pledged to do whatever he could to help them solve the case. The fact that he was willing to help made both

Babby and Laney feel even more certain that he wasn't guilty. He hadn't provided much in the way of useful information yet, but he did inform them that the charges from Evelyn's card all those years ago were for The Country Store - the oldest store in Evergreen. It wasn't until Laney plugged the name of the store into her map app that she saw the picture of the front of the building and recognized it.

"Wait, I know this place," she told Babby, just before they pulled out of the parking lot to follow Henry.

Laney zoomed in on the picture until she could make out the wooden sign that she had seen just that past weekend with Raymond. It was the store that they had stopped at twice during their ill-fated hiking trip. The friendly shopkeeper had mentioned that his place was the closest tourist spot to Centennial Woods.

"Is something wrong?" Babby asked.

Laney tapped the start button for directions.

"No, it's just strange to think that I was there twice, just last weekend."

She shuddered at the thought that the store that she had been in was one of the last stops that Evelyn had made while she was still alive. It was a sobering thought – a young woman had been shopping for souvenirs one moment and was gone the next. The thought made Laney even more determined to get to the bottom of the case.

They followed Henry Dale's pickup truck down the street to The Country Store. According to the internet listing, the store would be closing at eight-thirty, so they should have some time to check things out before they had to leave for the night. Henry seemed confident that they'd get plenty of information from the shop owner, an old friend of his. Laney knew that he was obviously referring to the amiable older man who had helped her and Raymond, which made her even more curious as to how he might be involved in everything. After pulling into a spot near the entrance of the charming little store, Laney hurried to follow Babby, who had practically leapt from the car before it even stopped moving. They met up with Henry at the door.

"Ed is a buddy of mine from college," he said. "This store has been in his family for as long as I can remember. I'm pretty sure he took it over from his dad about twenty-five years ago," he commented, opening the door, and standing back so that the ladies could enter the warmth of the shop.

"That's right around when Evelyn went missing, isn't it?" Babby asked.

Henry nodded gravely. "His dad actually worked with the cops back then to get those charges from Evelyn's bank account, but nothing conclusive came out of it. Ed was just getting ready to take over the store, but his dad was trying to protect him from all the craziness of the investigation. He seemed so scared, but now I'm wondering if he was more involved than he let on."

Laney's brows rose. Had Henry just thrown his life-long friend under the bus? "You think Ed had something to do with Evelyn going missing?" she asked, in a low voice.

"I'm honestly not sure of anything right now." Henry sighed. "But I think I know how we can find out. Just follow my lead." He strode toward the checkout counter, with Laney and Babby at his heels.

"Henry!? Is that you?" Ed called out from behind the counter.

He quickly abandoned his post to greet his friend when he saw that it indeed was Henry Dale visiting his shop. Henry smiled and reached out to shake hands, but Ed came in for a big hug instead. "Haven't seen you in a while- what's it been like six months, a year?"

Henry returned the friendly embrace with a solid clap on the shoulder. "I know, it's that whole working for a living thing that gets in the way." He chuckled.

"And we work right down the road from each other. It's crazy that we can't even find time for a coffee. We've gotta do better with that, my friend." Ed gave Henry a delighted smile, then looked past him, noticing Laney and Babby. "Well, hello ladies. Did you need help finding something?" He beamed.

Henry interjected before Babby or Laney could say a word. "Actually, Eddy, they're with me. This is Babby and Laney from over in Iberden." He nodded at them in turn as he made the introductions. Ed studied Laney then snapped his fingers.

"Hey, I remember you." He smiled. "You were here over the weekend with that tall guy. Hiking at the waterfall, right?" It was half a question, half a statement. "You guys come back for another trail?" He looked over her shoulder as if expecting Raymond to appear.

"Actually..." Laney glanced at Henry before proceeding and when he gave her a quick nod, she dove right in. "Babby and I came up here to meet with Henry because we thought he might be able to help us with something related to last weekend. He graciously offered to introduce us to you because he thought you'd have more information for us."

"Hmm, now I'm interested." Ed's brows rose. He looked to Henry for an explanation.

"You have a few minutes, Ed?" Henry asked, looking around the store to make sure that they weren't keeping Ed from helping customers. "I think it might help to give you some context about what we're asking"

"Sure, sure," Ed agreed. "Got all the time in the world. I was planning on closing up soon anyhow. Can you believe I haven't had a customer in the past hour?"

He walked back to the counter and gestured to a couple of well-worn plaid easy chairs that were in front of it. "Make yourselves comfortable, ladies, while Henry brings me up to speed. Go ahead now." He nodded at Henry. "Shoot."

Laney thought Henry was going to tread lightly, but subtlety didn't seem to be his strong suit.

"What do you remember about that case of the missing girl from Iberden? Back in the 90s?" he asked, sounding rather gruff.

Laney was shocked by his tone and Ed seemed taken aback too but recovered his smile quickly enough.

"Dad was running the store back then." Ed crossed his arms and frowned, seemingly trying to remember. "I remember that the cops came by the store a bunch and Dad helped them out with some administrative stuff. He didn't really share the details with me." He shrugged as if that settled it. "Why? What's up?"

"There's some new evidence," Henry began. "As of this past weekend, actually, when Laney was up here hiking."

A strange look passed over Ed's features so fleetingly that Laney wasn't certain she'd seen it at all, and she certainly couldn't interpret it. Fear? Anger?

"Really?" Ed's brows rose. "I thought they closed that case up a while ago. Didn't know anyone was still looking into it. What'd they find?"

Laney detected something 'off' in his tone. Could it be a hint of worry? She also noted that he was fidgeting with his hands, but his eyes were on Henry.

"Remains," Henry replied. "From the girl - Evelyn. Over on a trail at one of the parks."

Babby was clearly unable to stay quiet for a second longer and interrupted, "Oh, Ed, did you know Evelyn?"

"Umm..." Ed hesitated. "Uh, no, I don't think I knew much about her." He shook his head.

"She was actually like a daughter to me back in the day," Babby said sadly. "When I found out that Laney had discovered human remains, I was quite distraught, of course. They never found conclusive evidence that she had been killed, so I'd held on to hope over the years. As strange as it may sound, I always hoped that she had just run away and was safe somewhere, enjoying a new life."

She rose from her chair, drawing herself up to her full five feet, two inches. "And please excuse me, but

I'm not buying your story about not knowing much about the case. Your dad was heavily involved with the investigation, specifically because the last charges to Evelyn's credit card were from here."

Ed's face flushed and a vein throbbed at his temple. "What are you insinuating?" he asked quietly, stepping toward Babby, his hands clenched into fists at his sides. "I worked hard, even back then. Do you think that I would just follow some girl to the woods and kill her behind a waterfall?"

Babby didn't back down an inch. Ed might be big, but when Babby was all riled up about something, she was a force with which to be reckoned. She was about to give the much larger man what-for, when Henry stepped between them and held up his hands.

"Eddy, I wanna help you, I really do. But Babby deserves to know what really happened to her friend. If you know something…"

"I told you once, and I don't feel the need to tell you again…I don't know anything about what happened." He gritted his teeth for a moment, then closed his eyes and took a deep breath. When he opened his eyes, he gave Henry a look that was as dark as night. "This was a nice trip down memory lane, friend, but I think you should take the ladies and leave, now. "

Henry nodded. "You're right. It's not our job to get involved here. We'll leave this to the detectives. But just know that I'm telling them what I've gathered from this conversation."

"You've got nothing on me," Ed rasped. He looked pointedly at the door.

Laney and Babby followed Henry Dale outside quietly, each wondering what in the heck they were supposed to do now.

CHAPTER FOURTEEN

Once they were at the back of the parking lot, unlocking their cars, Laney wanted to ask a million questions, but before she could get a word out, Henry held a finger up to silence her.

"Go home. Or at least go back wherever you're staying the night, and if I were you two, I'd lock the doors and windows and check 'em twice," he advised, sending chills down Laney's spine.

Babby tried to argue but Henry wouldn't have it.

"I'm calling Detective Worth as soon as I get home tonight. I think I have enough info to make some pretty good guesses about what happened, but I can tell you right now she's not going to appreciate the fact that you two got so involved."

"But Ed didn't admit to anything." Babby sighed.

"Not directly," Henry clarified. "But you have to trust me. The tragedy happened in my jurisdiction, and I'll take care of it. You two need to get out of here. I'll reach out as soon as I have news."

Laney didn't entirely trust Henry. Frankly, she was actually beginning to wonder if his take-charge overly-helpful attitude was all just an act. It would be easy enough to find out. For now, she and Babby could get some sleep, and in the morning, a quick call to Detective Worth would let them know whether or not Henry had been on the up and up.

"Babby," Laney interjected, pulling on Babby's coat sleeve before the older woman embarked upon a tirade. "Let's go back to the B&B."

"But…" Babby tried to argue.

"It's okay." Laney gave her a look that said she'd tell her more later. "It's going to be okay. Let's just go for now. It's freezing out here."

Babby clamped her lips together, looking as though she might explode, but Laney calmly stared her down.

"Fine," Babby finally relented, looking weary. "But this isn't going to be the last that Ed hears from me. Not by a long shot."

Laney opened her door and Babby got in, refusing to even look in Henry's direction.

"Have a good night, Laney." He raised a hand in farewell.

"You too, Henry," Laney replied, not quite meeting his eyes.

She understood completely how Babby felt. They didn't know who to trust and hadn't gotten much further at all in their investigation. Both women were frustrated and drained, and the ride back to The Evergreen was a quiet one.

"Babby, I know that tonight didn't go exactly as we had planned, but I want you to know that I think we've found our guy," Laney said quietly, before they went upstairs to their rooms.

"Oh, for crying out loud, it could be either one of them." Babby made a face and waved her hand.

"Nope, it can't." Laney shook her head.

Babby's eyes widened. "What do you mean? If you know something that I don't know, young lady, you need to spit it out."

"Ed is the killer," Laney declared, without the slightest bit of doubt.

"And how, pray tell, do you happen to know that? I mean really...Ed? He's a nice guy who just got nervous when he was being questioned by his friend and two total strangers." Babby folded her arms across her chest.

"I thought about our conversation while I was driving. When Henry asked him if he knew anything, Ed specifically mentioned that Evelyn had been killed behind the waterfall," Laney explained patiently.

"Yeah, so?" Babby frowned, listening.

"So, the police never released that detail to the public. The only ones who knew about the location, outside of law enforcement, were Raymond and me.

If Ed knew where the remains were found without being told..." Laney gave Babby a meaningful look.

"Then that means that Ed is the killer," Babby murmured, her face going slack. "That horrible man killed my Evelyn," she blurted, bursting into tears.

Laney and Babby sat at a breakfast table at The Evergreen, with the Burlington News between them. They had both read the front-page story, in full, over and over, but they just couldn't look away from Ed's mug shot that was plastered above the story, front and center. The silence in the little bed and breakfast was deafening, as residents and visitors came to grips with the fact that there had been a killer living in the midst of their mountain paradise for quite some time.

Babby put down her coffee mug and cleared her throat. Laney turned to follow Babby's gaze and saw Henry Dale and Detective Worth standing in the foyer. Henry smiled and waved, but Worth had the annoyed look that she always seemed to get when facing Laney. Assuming that she was about to get scolded yet again by the detective, Laney took a breath and steeled herself for the onslaught, but when Worth reached their small table in the corner she simply grabbed the empty chair and took a seat between Laney and Babby. Henry remained standing, hovering over the detective's shoulder. When Laney met his gaze, he smiled and gave her two thumbs up. Laney and Babby both grinned in reply and Worth spoke.

"So, I understand that we have you two to thank for closing this twenty year old cold case?" She raised her eyebrows, but Laney and Babby stayed silent. Neither wanted to admit that they had meddled in a case that the detective had specifically warned them to stay away from.

Finally, Laney spoke, "We were just in the right place at the right time, I guess." She shrugged.

"Sure, you were," Detective Worth said dryly. "But, what's done is done. I see you've read the paper?"

Laney and Babby nodded in unison, and Worth turned to Babby, her expression softening a bit. "So, you got the answers that you needed?" she asked the older woman.

Unable to speak, Babby swallowed hard and nodded, dropping her gaze as she tried to hold herself together.

"Good." Worth stood and shook hands with both of them, much to Laney's surprise. "Thank you," the detective said. "Both of you. As much as I hate to say it, we wouldn't have gotten to the bottom of this so quickly without your help."

"Well, he and Henry were friends. Without Henry's help we couldn't have had the conversation that we did with him."

Worth nodded. "Getting him to reveal that he knew the location of the remains was the key to being able to arrest him. We have plenty of other evidence, but that was definitely the icing on the cake. You did well, Laney. Now, for the love of all that is holy, stop poking your nose where it doesn't belong. Are we clear on that?" Worth asked, staring Laney down.

"Crystal clear. I hope I never encounter another murder case as long as I live." Laney blew out a breath.

"I thought it was kind of fun." Babby had a wicked gleam in her eye.

"Don't even think about it," Worth warned, jabbing a finger in Babby's direction.

They all laughed, and the detective left.

"I still can't believe it." Henry shook his head slowly. "I never would've thought that Ed would be capable of something like this. I still don't even know what the motive was. He wouldn't admit to anything, but obviously once they knew where to start looking they found enough to charge him."

"I know what the motive was," Babby said softly.

Laney and Henry turned to her, eyes wide.

"What? Babby, is there something that you haven't been telling us?" Laney asked.

Babby nodded.

"When Evelyn worked for me, she kept a little locked box that she called her treasure chest. She showed it to me and told me that if anything ever happened to her, she wanted me to have the chest, but that I shouldn't open it unless I absolutely had to. I told her she was being silly, of course. What could possibly happen to a young, beautiful girl, right?" Babby shook her head and dashed a hand across her eyes.

"It was almost like she knew. Anyway, when we figured out who the killer was last night, I went into the trunk of my car and pulled out the box. I opened it with the key that she kept in the cash drawer of the register, and inside I found dozens and dozens of letters…from Ed. He'd written to her and told her that he loved her, over and over, but she'd refused him. There were threats, followed by apologies…the last one is dated right before her death. He invited her up to talk. He wanted to take her behind the waterfall for privacy."

Babby lowered her head and covered her face with her hands, her bony shoulders shaking with sobs. Laney scooted her chair over and placed an arm around her friend. Babby shook her head and took several deep breaths to try and pull herself together.

"Babby, you need to get those letters to Detective Worth," Henry said softly. "Why didn't you do that while she was here?"

Babby gazed up at him, her eyes bleary with tears.

"It's the last little piece of Evelyn that I have, and when I turn it in to Worth, it'll go in a cold, dreary evidence room and I'll never see it again. I just wanted to hold onto it for a little while longer. I'll take it to Worth when I go back into town."

"Babby, as much as it'll hurt to let that go, you'll know that you've helped to put her killer behind bars," Laney said, hugging the older woman.

Babby pulled back and looked at Laney, her expression bitter.

"Yes, and if I hadn't been a sentimental old fool, I would've looked in that darn box when she went missing and Ed would've been locked up twenty-five years ago."

You could have heard a pin drop in that breakfast room.

"Welp, better late than never," Henry proclaimed, and Laney had never felt so relieved in her entire life.

ALSO BY SUMMER PRESCOTT

Check out all the books in Summer Prescott's catalog!

Summer Prescott Book Catalog

AUTHOR'S NOTE

I'd love to hear your thoughts on my books, the storylines, and anything else that you'd like to comment on—reader feedback is very important to me. My contact information, along with some other helpful links, is listed on the next page. If you'd like to be on my list of "folks to contact" with updates, release and sales notifications, etc.... just shoot me an email and let me know. Thanks for reading!

Also...

... if you're looking for more great reads, Summer Prescott Books publishes several popular series by outstanding Cozy Mystery authors.

CONTACT SUMMER PRESCOTT BOOKS PUBLISHING

Twitter: @summerprescott1

Bookbub: https://www.bookbub.com/authors/summer-prescott

Blog and Book Catalog: http://summerprescottbooks.com

Email: summer.prescott.cozies@gmail.com

YouTube: https://www.youtube.com/channel/UCngKNUkDdWuQ5k7-Vkfrp6A

And...be sure to check out the Summer Prescott Cozy Mysteries fan page and Summer Prescott Books Publishing Page on Facebook – let's be friends!

CONTACT SUMMER PRESCOTT BOOKS PUBLISHING

To download a free book, and sign up for our fun and exciting newsletter, which will give you opportunities to win prizes and swag, enter contests, and be the first to know about New Releases, click here: http://summerprescottbooks.com

Printed in Great Britain
by Amazon